Dear Bethany,
One of the sweetest
gals I know you in
God bless you in
all of your future
endeavors. Love,
Sis Chipp

STONESTHROW

NIKKI PRESCOTT

PublishAmerica
Baltimore

At the specific preference of the author, PublishAmerica allowed this work to remain exactly as the author intended, verbatim, without editorial input.

ISBN: 1-4241-9213-7
PUBLISHED BY PUBLISHAMERICA, LLLP
www.publishamerica.com
Baltimore

Printed in the United States of America

FOR MY THREE LOVES

Acknowledgments

I would especially like to thank Zack, my husband of fifty-one years, and our two sons, Frank and Jon, whose encouragement and support went above and beyond. Bob, my editor/brother, who has always urged me to try a little harder. The Great Smoky Mountains National Park Service whose historical information was of major importance. Kaye, whose friendship has been never-failing, all of the Tennessee residents we are privileged to call our friends, and Miss Keating, who started it all a long, long time ago.

Bobby watched his father put on his tie.

"Aren't you going to school today?"

"Nae." Henry put his jacket on. As he buttoned it, he said, "Your Mom and I are meeting with the landlord, Mr. McPhee, about buying this house. I think we rented it long enough."

"I guess you will be studying with Professor Jameson for a long time, then?"

Bobby had been very young when they came to Leith from England, but he'd heard the story often enough, about how his dad had wanted to study chemistry but had changed to geology, just like Professor Robert Jameson, of Edinburgh University, and moved his family to Leith to study with the master. He had become the professor's star pupil and expected to work with him when he was through with his courses.

"Aye. No school for you, today, either. We'd like you to do us a favor. The professor lent me some papers to study over the weekend and I'd like you to return them for me."

Bobby's parents had seen to it that he'd been well educated. He spoke English, albeit with a heavy brogue, perfect French, and he was learning Scottish Gaelic. His real talent was in mathematics and he was on his way to earning an important scholarship. He could afford a day off.

"It's a long walk," his dad continued, "so here's some money for lunch."

7

Bobby took the money and gave his Mom a kiss on the cheek.

As he left, he heard his dad ask her where his new cufflinks were.

"They're upstairs," she answered. "I put them in your cupboard."

"I'll come with you."

These were the last words Bobby ever heard his father say.

The professor's secretary, Mrs. McDonald, was almost as old as the professor, and had worked for him since he joined the staff.

"How've you been, Bobby?"" She spoke in precise Scottish Gaelic.

"I'm fine, Mrs. McDonald, but I am still learning Gaelic, so it may be better if we talk English today."

He is a lovely boy, thought Mrs. McDonald, so mannerly and polite and handsome too, with that silver-blond hair. He's going to please a lot of ladies. Aloud, she teased, "There's nothing wrong with that brogue, though. It won't be long until you're rattling off the true tongue. I'll see that Professor Jameson gets these. "

Bobby smiled, and headed home. Along the way, he stopped in at the bakery and bought a scone to eat as he walked.

When he arrived, he was shocked to see a tragic scene. Neighbors, and people he'd never seen before, were all at his house, which was still smoldering.

"What?" He couldn't speak. "My mom and dad," he let out a whimper.

"Sorry, Laddie. We couldn't get to them. They were trapped upstairs when sparks fell from the fireplace, and caught the mat on the floor. The place went up like a tinderbox. They had no chance." It was Mr. McPhee, the landlord.

Bobby sat down in the street, as the crowd began to disperse. He couldn't think.

8

Mr. McPhee put his hand on his shoulder and told him that he could come home with him for the night. Bobby went quietly, not willing to let what happened sink in just yet.

In the morning, Professor Jameson sent a carriage for Bobby, with an invitation to stay as long as he'd like. Bobby thanked Mr. McPhee and left, still not sure of the previous day's horror. When he arrived at the professor's, he discovered that the great man had taken a day off from school to receive him.

"You can stay here as long as you like, young Bobby." The professor was now a widower, so his housekeeper, elderly Miss Barbara, was there to carry out the professor's orders. "Miss Barbara will get you some clothing and shoes, show you where you'll sleep, and I think you'll need some sustenance, too. I'll bet you haven't eaten since yesterday." The professor's eyes were kind and sympathetic.

"Thank you, Sir." Bobby could say no more as the reality of the shock began to overtake him. The boy's body shuddered and he began to cry with large sobs and moans. Tears fell, unashamedly, and he sat down on the nearest chair. Miss Barbara went over to him and hugged him to her matronly figure, her own tears quietly falling.

She let him cry a few minutes before she said, "Come on, Laddie, I have a big breakfast waiting for you in the kitchen. After that, you can have a nice warm bath and a nap. That'll help. And then, you can talk with the professor."

The kind woman gently helped him rise and walked him to the kitchen. He was still crying as she ushered him to a place at the large table in the kitchen where several cooks who were preparing lunch choked up when they saw him, knowing what had taken place. In no time at all, one of the men put a steaming cup of tea in front of him. In a few minutes there was a plate of sausages, eggs, toast and a platter of scones, with jam and butter to go with them. He hadn't realized how hungry he was, and he managed to get quite a bit of it down before the tears came again.

While he napped, Miss Barbara sent out for clothes and shoes, and when he awoke they were all laid out on a chair near his bed. He dressed and returned to the professor's parlor where he found the compassionate gentleman reading.

"Ah, Bobby!" Professor Jameson put his book down and pointed to a chair. "Are you well enough now to make some decisions?"

"Aye, Sir," Bobby said, as he sat. "Thank you for the clothes and the shoes. They fit well." He studied the pattern in the carpet, deeply saddened by the events.

"Well, young man, you're welcome to come here and live with me. Your father was my prize pupil and I admired his interest and his work ethic. I'm sure you have inherited his good behavior. You may even study with me when you're older, if you wish. I would be delighted to have you follow in his footsteps."

Bobby was overwhelmed. Things were going too fast. "Thank you, Professor. I haven't had much time to think about it, now, but I have often considered going to Alloa to work in either the mines or the breweries. They seem to pay well from what I've heard."

"I wouldn't want you to do that, Son. Why use your back when you have a good brain?" The professor's argument made sense. "You have an education and it wouldn't take much studying to put you at the head of any class you chose."

"Then," it came out of nowhere, "I think I would like to go to America." Bobby surprised himself. As he thought about it some more it seemed to be the right thing to do. "I don't think I should stay here and be reminded of my dear parents every day. I don't think I could bear it. Yes! That's what I'll do. Go to America." He smiled for the first time in two days.

"Are you sure I can't change your mind?" The professor could tell it may be the best way for the boy to cope with the shock of losing his family.

"No, I think not." Bobby had some money in the bank. His father had seen to it that he'd been thrifty and taught him to save at an early age. He wasn't sure if it would be enough for the voyage but it would help.

"If you don't mind me staying here until I get a ship, I would be grateful."

"My Boy, I said you might stay here as long as you like. Now, if you are set on this adventure, I know a ship captain. He is Captain R. Spittal. Right now, he just runs from Leith to Alloa, but I will send him a message to send us the name of a trans-Atlantic captain who will take you on. I'm sure you will make, at the very least, an honest and able cabin boy."

"Until we can co-ordinate things do you want to come and do some filing for me at the University? I have some paperwork that needs to be put in order. I am notorious as far as filing properly, and I know Mrs. McDonald is grossly overworked."

"Begging your pardon, Sir, I'm afraid to look at my dear dad's place would only break my heart again. Are there some chores I can do for you here, at home?" The boy was hopeful.

"Of course how insensitive of me. I'm sure Miss Barbara could use a hand fetching and lifting heavy items. If you don't mind that can be your task while you are here. And if she doesn't need you, please feel free to explore my library. Just be sure to make yourself at home."

"Thank you, Sir." Bobby was, indeed, grateful to the kindly old man, and knew why his father had held him in such high esteem. He had the gift of making one feel capable and confident.

The next afternoon, Bobby used one of the professor's many carriages to take him to the waterfront to look for Captain Spittal. It was the day of his return trip from Alloa and Bobby was glad to be ushered into the messiest office he had ever seen. There were stacks and stacks of paper everywhere. The captain was trying to sort through them.

When Bobby gave him the note, he sat up straight, still holding a pile of papers with his other hand. His hat was pushed back and Bobby noticed he had a big, friendly smile.

"How is the professor?" He also had great admiration for the man who was the Regius Professor of Natural History at Edinburgh University. Everyone in Leith knew of him and admired him.

"He's fine." Bobby looked around for a chair but they were all full of papers. "He thought that maybe you could suggest a ship going to America."

"Where do you want to go? North? South? Where?" The captain started rifling through the papers he still held.

"I have no idea, Sir. What do you advise?"

"If I were moving to America I would head south. I hear the climate is warmer, there."

"Then, south it is." Bobby was relieved to meet someone who knew about this faraway place he'd only heard his father speak of in conversations with friends or neighbors.

Captain Spittal pulled a paper out of the stack he had in his hand. "Here's something. The HMS Rainbow. It will leave on the thirty-first of March for Savannah, Georgia. Can't say I blame the captain for choosing that date. That way, most of the violent north Atlantic storms have passed and you should have a good trip. The captain is a good friend of mine, Captain Heigham. He'll take good care of you. The fact that you can read and write will also please him. You'll be able to lighten his bookkeeping and log-listing chores. He happens to be staying at the Dry Duck Hotel right now, so I'll give you a note to bring over there. Good luck to you, Laddie."

Bobby thanked the captain and headed for the hotel. He was familiar with the place. It had been built on the edge of a bulkhead right near the mouth of the Water of Leith, and he often sat on the wooden railing in the back to watch the ships take off for ports all over the world.

There was a small café in the lobby and Bobby spied the captain right away. He was sitting alone, having coffee, and checking the large barometer, which hung on the wall by the window for all to see. He looked up when Bobby approached him.

"Please, Sir, I have a note here from Captain Spittal." He handed it to the man, held his breath, and awaited his reply.

"Well, Bobby, you come highly recommended, and I am in need of a cabin boy. What will you do when you get to America, stay or return?"

"Please, Sir, I plan to stay. There is nothing here for me to return to so I will seek my fortune there."

The captain liked the young man's polite manner and realized he had had an education. He would be an asset. "I'm only sorry you won't be coming back with us. You sound like someone I could really use. Nevertheless," he stood up and shook Bobby's hand, "welcome aboard. Be here in three days. We sail at dawn."

The three days he spent at the professor's went quickly and it was time to go. Both Miss Barbara and the professor had become fond of him as they got to know him better and told him he would be missed. He knew in his heart he would miss them, too.

Bobby shook the professor's hand. Miss Barbara gave him a bear hug and called him "her dear boy," and he felt tears on her cheeks as he backed away. He climbed into the carriage, put the small case carrying his new clothes on his lap, and waved goodbye, as the driver turned the rig toward the waterfront.

It was just before dawn when he arrived at the ship. Although a heavy mist still enveloped the pier, the sailors were bustling about. Bobby felt the element of excitement in the air, and was thrilled to be a part of it. He stood at the gangplank, just watching, until he was almost knocked over by a burly man, whom he learned later was called, "Big Vic."

The voyage was uneventful as far as the weather was concerned. Bobby felt torn, some days, trying to decide if he should become a sailor, or explore America.

The captain treated him well. He found the bookkeeping interesting and the sea was enticing. His only problem was at night when he slept in the sailors' bunk.

Big Vic, a huge, muscular man, with a vulgar mouth, seemed to constantly pick on Bobby, and Bobby often had to duck to avoid being slapped or punched. He had no idea why Big Vic hated him so much. The other sailors all thought it was funny, but Bobby spent many a night huddled in his bunk, afraid to go to sleep, especially when he knew Big Vic had had more than he should have had of rum.

One morning, after a particularly scary night Bobby yawned so much, the captain noticed.

"Why are you so tired, my Boy?"

Bobby didn't want to tell on Big Vic, but he had had so many sleepless nights being afraid of being thrown overboard, or killed, that he admitted to having trouble with one of the men. He didn't name him but the captain guessed who it was.

"Starting tonight, you can sleep up here in my cabin on the couch. I can't have my chief bookkeeper falling asleep on the job." He smiled.

The rest of the trip went well, as Bobby completely avoided Big Vic, who, unknown to Bobby, was even angrier and more jealous of him.

Savannah was a welcome sight. Bobby had thought the port of Leith had been bustling! That was nothing compared to this. There were many ships here with English, French and Spanish names. There were, as he discovered later, slave traders, carrying human cargo, and spice ships from the Orient, as well as ships full of all kinds of materials and passengers from many countries. It was a remarkable place.

"I'm going to miss you, Lad. Is there is a way to change your mind?" The captain looked hopefully at Bobby.

"No, Sir, but I thank you for all you've taught me and all you've done for me. I'll go to the dock registrar to see if I can get some work loading ships for awhile until I learn more about this great country." He shook the captain's hand and left the ship.

In his pocket he had a letter of recommendation from the captain to give to Amos Scudder, the owner of the Ogeechie canal, who transported timber, rice, shingles and tobacco to the Savannah River. Captain Heigham knew one of the barge captains who worked for him and thought that Bobby might get hired there until he decided on his next move. Bobby applied at the office only to be told that Captain Fultze was over at the restaurant.

It was almost twilight when Bobby got to the restaurant. It was starting to fill up with sailors and dockworkers, and when Bobby entered, he had no idea who Captain Fultze was. He asked the lady at the door who seemed to be a proprietor and she pointed to a man, eating heartily, at a table next to the side door.

"Excuse me, Sir. Are you Captain Fultze?"

"Yeah! Who wants to know?" The man's gruff voice surprised Bobby, who, except for Big Vic, had only met kind people since he left home.

"Captain Heigham sent this note for either you or Mr. Scudder," he gave the man the note. "I would like to know if you are hiring."

The captain looked up for the first time. "You? Don't make me laugh. You're just a slip of a kid. You can't help me. What the devil's Heigham sending me, now? You look like a stiff wind would blow you over." He resumed eating, after telling Bobby to be on his way.

Unsure of what to do next, Bobby left the restaurant through the side door, which brought him into a long alley. He didn't know which direction to take when he heard a chilling voice.

"There you are, you little runt. Things were all right until you came along. My nephew had that job sewed up until you brought all those fancy letters from high people. They won't help you now. I'll finish the job I should have finished on the ship."

Big Vic was very drunk, and in his hand was a baling hook, the kind used to pick up bulky items on a loading dock. He swung and missed.

Bobby turned to see if anyone was there that could help him, but no one was. As he turned back toward Vic the hook caught him in his right eye and he crumpled to the ground.

Seeing the blood, Big Vic fled, throwing the hook away as he ran, thinking he had killed the boy.

Holding his bleeding eye, Bobby stumbled back to the side door of the restaurant and fell inside. The proprietor rushed to help and she had two strong patrons carry Bobby down the street to the doctor's. The doctor tended him as well as he could but there was no saving the eye. He put him to bed, used whiskey to sedate him, and removed what was left of the damaged eye. Bobby went into shock and the doctor didn't think he would make it, but after a few days of intensive nursing, Bobby pulled through.

When he was well enough to leave the doctor's, Bobby, now wearing a black patch over that eye, decided to get as far away from the waterfront as possible. He had had several conversations with the doctor's aide as he recovered, and learned there had been a gold rush in northern Georgia. The excitement of possibly striking it rich tempted him as much as it had men twice his age, so he decided to make his way there.

He left Savannah, walking in a generally northwestern direction. By the first nightfall, he was on a deserted road, so he sat beside a huge Live Oak tree dripping with moss, and slept there. In the morning, he continued on, coming upon a farmhouse where a man was outside, chopping wood.

"Hey, Young Man, whither are you bound?" The man came over to Bobby, offering his hand as he stared at his eye patch. "What happened, Young Sir?"

"An accident," Bobby lied.

"Well, we are just about to sit down to breakfast. Come in and join us, Young Sir, before you go on your way." He put his arm around Bobby' shoulder and led him into the house.

"Bessie, come and see. We have a young sir to join us this morning."

His rotund little wife, wearing a polka-dot scarf on her head, came into the room, wiping her hands on her apron. She had a broad smile until she saw the patch on his eye.

"Oh, you poor dear." She ushered Bobby to the table. As he sat she told him, "I'll have your food, straightaway, Young Sir."

She scurried into the kitchen and came back with a heaping platter of eggs and bacon, and a tray full of muffins and pancakes. The aroma alone made Bobby very hungry and he realized he hadn't eaten for quite awhile.

He enjoyed the meal and when he was finished asked if he could pay them for it, but they insisted it was their privilege to have the company of such a fine young man. They said their goodbyes and he was on his way. As he walked, he met many such kind hosts, who gave him food and, often, shelter for the night, and not one of them would accept any payment for their generosity.

He reached the town known as Licklog around a month after he left Savannah. It was the end of eighteen forty-seven, and the gold was beginning to peter out. He had heard of the Trail of Tears from one of the farmers who put him up for the night. He learned that the Cherokees had been forced to relocate since they had occupied most of the land in the gold region.

Once again, as he had been at the sight of the slave ships at the port in Savannah as they unloaded their unhappy cargo, he was sickened by the thought of man's inhumanity to man. He had come from a free, civilized society and could not relate to the awful idea of Manifest Destiny, or people owning other people. He was beginning to fantasize about living all alone in this barbaric area. Surely, he would be able to find a way to support himself without getting too close to anyone.

He found a hotel in town and signed up at the bathhouse. The man who came in after him was a tall, scruffy, dirty fellow, with a long, thick beard. At first, his booming voice and arrogant swagger intimidated Bobby.

"What have we here? A mere boy. A child," he laughed, and added something in a foreign tongue, which Bobby recognized as French.

"Don't know, Sir."

At this, the man roared with laughter. "Listen to that brogue," he said aloud, although no one else was in the room. "Now, would we have a little Scotsman here?"

Bobby answered him in perfect French.

"I come from across the ocean the same as you, Sir, to seek my fortune in this place, but I cannot abide the cruelty I find in the inhabitants and wonder if I have made a dreadful mistake."

The Frenchman was taken aback and smiled, as he let out a wild yell. "He speaks French." To Bobby, he said, "Where did you learn that?"

"From my dear parents. They believed in education." Bobby no longer feared the man He was beginning to enjoy his loud and boisterous ways.

"And where are these wonderful parents? And why do you wear that patch?" The mountain man had been washing all this time and was beginning to look quite decent.

Bobby answered, "They are deceased, Sir, and the patch is to cover up an eye I lost in a waterfront attack."

"Do you mean you've come all the way from Scotland all alone, and have no kin here?"

"Aye, Sir." Bobby was finished washing, so he got up and started to dry himself. "I have no further plans. I thought I might pan for gold but one of the prospectors told me the gold is beginning to slow down, so I have to try to think of what else I can do."

"What's your name, Boy?"

"Robert Cutter, but I am called Bobby."

"How'd you like to learn to trap? There's a good living in it and I could use the help. I have too many traps to check them all, myself. By the way, my name is Pierre LaRue, but you can call me Pete."

"I don't know anything about trapping," Bobby admitted.

"Are you willing to learn, Boy?"

"Why, yes, I suppose so." Bobby liked the idea of being in the company of this big Frenchman. He seemed to be friendly enough and would offer him some protection from danger.

"Then, it's settled. We'll leave tomorrow morning for my cabin up north."

At the first trickle of daylight, Bobby woke, in the hotel's lumpy four-poster. He jumped into his clothes, gathered up his things and raced downstairs to the café, to find Pete wolfing down some pancakes.

"Good afternoon," Pete teased. The great man's voice resounded throughout the room and the other diners laughed. "No need to worry, my Boy, I would have come to get you. Have some breakfast."

The waitress served Bobby some coffee and a heaping plate of pancakes. He ate quickly and they were soon ready to leave.

Pete had a mule-driven wagon, which was all ready for them when they reached the livery stable. As they rode, the stunning scenery transformed Bobby. There were mountains and valleys and more mountains, as far as he could see. He felt in his heart and soul that this was the place he wanted to be.

Late in the afternoon, they reached a clearing at the top of a steep ridge. There was a small wooden cabin, a lean-to, and a shed for the mule.

"Here we are," Pete said, as he jumped down from the wagon, led the mule to a hitching post and began to remove the harness.

Bobby sat in the wagon a few moments, looking around in every direction. The view was breathtaking.

"This is incredible."

"Let's get in and get some grub. I'm hungry." Pete led the way into the cabin.

It was small and sparsely furnished. There were animal skin rugs on the one bed, and also a hand-built table and two chairs.

"We'll make you a bed in awhile," Pete said.

There was a rifle over the mantle and Pete asked Bobby if he knew how to shoot.

"No. My father was a university student. We lived in the city."

"Well, I'll teach you. There are still some marauders around here. That's why my cabin is built in this spot. It affords me circular vision so I can not be taken by surprise."

After a supper of beans and venison jerky, Pete nailed together some planks he had in the shed. Then, he stretched a huge deerskin rug over the space and laced it to the wood.

"Now, you have a bed." Pete said.

Bobby was amazed at his ingenuity.

The next few days were taken up setting traps and digging caches, which Bobby learned made the job easier in the long run. As they traveled over the ridges, they dug holes in certain marked spots, covered them with dirt and leaves so no one else could find them. That way, they wouldn't have to carry all of their pelts as they gathered them, but merely dig them up on the way back.

Bobby learned that there were twelve traps in a string; how to trap a beaver and stretch the pelt over willow branches to dry, and then pack it in a frame until there was a bale of fifty pelts. He dried venison by sticking the meat on an eight-foot high pole until it dried so he would have jerky to take along the trail with him. In spite of using only one eye, he became an excellent shot, and the years passed quickly.

He became quite tall and muscular as he aged, his body tanned and healthy. His silver-blond hair shone in the sunlight. He grew a beard for awhile but he found it itchy and annoying so he shaved it off and never grew it back.

Pete had told Bobby that he should expect it, and one day, a Cherokee warrior showed up at the cabin. Bobby learned his name was Strong Eagle and that he was a good friend to Pete. He brought them two rabbits and had dinner with them. Bobby was awed by his kindness, and the Indian was impressed that Bobby had come so far all alone, and with just one eye. He invited Bobby and Pete to his village, which was over the border in Tennessee.

Bobby learned that this particular band had avoided the Trail of Tears by hiding in the mountains until they were finally given their own land. They had a civilization that was on a par with any of the European settlements in the area, with houses, and books in their own written language. Bobby could never understand why the white men he met on his trips down the mountain to sell his furs called these hunters and gatherers "savages".

They visited frequently, until one day, Bobby was invited to move up to the Cherokee land. The Indians built him a cabin, where, like Pete's, it had a complete view of the surrounding area. He now had his own place, so Pete went back to Georgia, promising to come whenever he could.

By now, Bobby had become a proficient hunter and trapper, sometimes going by himself and other times, hunting with his Cherokee friends. They called him Sa-qu-i-u-Di-ga-to-li, or, One-eye. He loved his new life and was content to live in the mountains. It was the unique lifestyle he'd hoped to have in this new country.

On a trip to Townsend, Tennessee, Bobby headed for J.J. Phillips, Fur Trader, with a large frame of beaver pelts. He wore his usual mountain clothes: a coonskin cap, a deerskin jacket tied with latigo, long deerskin leggings and heavy leather boots. His tall, imposing physique might have been intimidating, especially with the black patch over one eye, but his voice was warm and friendly, and the combination of his Scottish brogue with a Tennessee drawl gave his words a charming lilt.

J.J.'s daughter, Annie. was in charge of the business that day and when she came around the counter she felt an immediate attraction to Bobby. He also felt it, and, in that first moment, he knew there had been something unknown missing in his life.

Bobby spoke first. "Is J.J. here?"

"No, I'm sorry. He's in Knoxville for a few days." She pretended to examine the pelts.

Bobby saw a slender woman of about twenty-five, wearing a white blouse with a black bowtie, and a long black skirt. She had chestnut brown hair, which was pinned up on her head, and had bright dark eyes and a charming smile.

"I'm Robert Cutter," he offered her his hand to shake.

She took it and he held hers longer than he had intended to as he looked into her eyes. Her smile captivated him.

She finally removed her hand and blushed as she went back behind the counter.

Bobby removed his cap, revealing a thick shock of silver-blond hair. She had told him her name was Annie and that she was J.J.'s daughter.

"I haven't been here before. I usually go to Cosby area, or Newport. A friend of mine told me that J.J. was a fair man, so I thought I'd come this way. If he likes these skins I can bring him many more."

"Where are you from?" Annie didn't want to end the conversation.

"I live with the Cherokees." Bobby felt self-conscious about his eye patch.

Annie must have felt his discomfort because she asked," What happened to your eye?"

"I had an accident when I was a boy." Bobby felt that any chance he had with her was finished. He put his cap back on and prepared to leave.

She leaned over the counter and put her hand on his arm.

"Wait," she asked, "will you be back?"

"If J.J. likes my pelts."

"Please don't think I'm being forward, but I'd like to see you again."

Bobby was rejuvenated by her remark. He looked into her eyes, finding encouragement and hope there.

"I can return in about a month, or so. It'll take me that long to get another frame full."

"Are you staying in town for now?" Annie had never done anything like this before but this handsome mountain man seemed warm and friendly.

"Yes. I'll be at the Apple Hotel for a day or so."

"Well, why don't you come for supper? When Dad is away my meals are lonely. I'd enjoy some company. I live upstairs. Shall we say about seven?" She shook his hand again He once again held her hand a second more than a perfunctory shake would take.

"I'd be honored, Ma'am." He went out into the sun, and headed for the hotel to take a bath and get cleaned up for the first date he'd ever had.

The evening couldn't come fast enough for Bobby. He stopped at the general store and bought a box of chocolates for Annie. He still wore the same clothes but he had washed and shaved and, without the coonskin cap he looked quite respectable.

Annie opened the door, and laughed as she ushered him into the living quarters. "You're right on time. Come on in." There was an elderly lady in the dining room, setting the table for two. She gave Bobby the once over and tried not to stare when she noticed his eye patch.

Annie guided him over to a chair next to the fireplace. "This is Mrs. Harding. She is my right arm. Don't know what we'd do without her." Bobby nodded to the lady who finished what she was doing and, after giving him a slight curtsey, went back into the kitchen.

He took the seat and Annie sat opposite in a wooden rocking chair.

"I hope you're hungry. Mrs. Harding made us a fine venison roast. But first, you must tell me, how did you ever get to Tennessee?"

Bobby related his life story up until now, feeling comfortable and satisfied to tell Annie everything. She leaned forward and listened intently.

When he had finished, he asked her, " Now, what about you?"

She laughed. He liked the sound of her laugh "There isn't much to tell. It's just my dad and I, since my mother passed away. She had Pneumonia when I was small and we lost her. He has taught me the business and feels that, if I were alone, I could take care of myself. Some say he's gruff and cranky but he is a fair man and, if you don't try to take advantage of him he will always treat you right."

"I was surprised to find you were unattached. In these mountains there seems to be early marriages."

"This is a small town and everyone knows everyone. I've been so busy helping my dad with the business, and I've watched my friends all pair off, but I haven't met anyone I want to settle down with." He couldn't miss the twinkle in her eye as she added," Yet." She laughed again, and took his arm to help him out of the chair.

"Let's eat."

Mrs. Harding had made a fine supper, and they ate heartily, Bobby noticing that Annie's appetite almost matched his. That pleased him. In fact, everything about Annie pleased him, and by the time the evening was over he realized he wanted her in his life from now on.

Annie sensed a feeling she had never known before, and didn't want Bobby to leave.

"My dad will be back tomorrow. Will you still be in town?"

"No. It's a day's journey to home and I have some other traps I need to check. I'll be back in about a month. Thank you so much for supper. Tell Mrs. Harding it was delicious."

In a spontaneous gesture he leaned over and pecked her on the cheek.

As she closed the door, she added, "Goodnight, Bobby Cutter. Come back soon."

Bobby felt exhilarated He had some trouble falling asleep that night and when he did he dreamed of Annie, coming out of his cabin on Cherokee Ridge, wearing an apron and smiling that charming smile of hers.

He left for home the next morning, thinking of Annie all the way there. The next month seemed to drag although Bobby set twice as many traps and framed twice as many beaver pelts to take to J.J. Phillips Fur Trader's. Annie often crept into his thoughts and he looked forward to seeing her again.

It was just a few days shy of exactly one month when Bobby loaded up his wagon with skins, hitched up his mule and told Strong Eagle he'd be back with a surprise. His friend had absolutely no idea that Bobby planned to propose to Annie on this visit.

When he reached the store, J.J. was behind the counter and Annie was nowhere to be seen. Bobby went in and introduced himself to J.J., a slight built baldheaded man with an unlit cigar hanging out of his mouth.

"You're the mountain man my daughter was telling me about. Those pelts you left were flawless, so I'd be glad to see what else you've brought." He removed the cigar while he spoke.

It was all business for a while, and after they attended to the details Bobby finally asked about Annie.

"She's down at the mercantile, shopping for some cloth. Says she wants a new dress, although I think she has enough dresses." J.J. suddenly added two and two together.

"I'm telling you, Mister, if you have any ideas about my daughter, you'd better forget them. There is no way in Hell I'll let her marry a mountain man. She has what she needs right here, without getting into a hard life up there, and, as she tells me, you live with the Indians, which is even worse."

Bobby recognized another prejudiced southerner. He knew Annie didn't feel that way. He could sense J.J. considered his eye patch another problem. He didn't want to argue, so he said goodbye and left.

He headed down the street to the store, almost bumping into Annie as she came out, carrying a bundle. He took the bundle from her, tipped his hat and said,

"I've missed you. How have you been?" He could feel the electricity between them.

Her smile was warm and wide. "Bobby. I missed you, too. Have you been to the store? Did you meet my dad?" They had stopped to chat at the corner.

"I did," He answered, a dark cloud coming over his face. "He said he wouldn't have you bothering with me, or any other mountain man."

"Poor Daddy. He has been alone so long, he depends on me. I doubt he'd want me to see anyone." She seemed puzzled as to what to do next.

"Dear Annie, I haven't thought of anything but you since we met, and I've come to ask you to be my wife. I know life gets tough in the mountains but I promise I will try to make it as easy as I can for you. And I will bring you into town whenever you like, to see your dad and shop, or whatever you want."

"I feel the same about you, Bobby. I'm so glad you've come into my life and, with your kind and gentle ways; I don't want to lose you. I would be honored to become your wife. Let's tell Daddy."

J.J. wouldn't hear of it. He ranted and raved, until Annie said, "Daddy, I love Bobby and he loves me, and we are going to be married, with your blessing or without it. I would hope you'd want me to be happy but if it has to be this way, so be it."

To Bobby, she said, "I'll pack my things and be right down. You can wait outside for me."

"If you leave, don't ever come back." J.J. was adamant.

Bobby went to the livery stable, got his mule and wagon and got back to the store just as Annie closed the door behind her, while J.J. was still yelling, "And don't come back!"

Annie climbed up into the wagon by Bobby's side and they headed up to Cherokee Ridge, their happiness marred by J.J.'s unpleasantness.

"You can stay with Strong Eagle and his wife until I can get a minister up there to marry us. You'll love these people as I do."

"I'm sure I will," Annie snuggled closer to Bobby, knowing she had done the right thing. After a few days, Bobby was able to have Reverend Horace Whitamore, from Cosby, come over and perform a wedding ceremony. Strong Eagle and his family attended, bringing many useful gifts. They had succeeded in reaching Pete, and, although he was a late arrival, Bobby was overjoyed to have the two loves in his life together at last.

Pete and Annie took to each other right away. The only blight on the day was that J.J. would not be there to attend his only daughter's happiest moment.

Annie grasped mountain life quickly. She learned to make homemade preserves, molasses, smoked meat, and taffy. She taught the Cherokee women her skills in sewing and quilting, and they taught her how to dry pelts and make clothing from the deerskins. She quilted during the long winter nights and tended a huge vegetable garden in the summer.

As much as Annie and Bobby hoped for children, none came. Annie finally admitted she was unable to have any, and often cried about it when Bobby was away collecting his pelts. Bobby didn't seem to mind it, except for the fact that he felt sad for Annie. The two of them grew more and more in love as time went by, and after six years, their lives had taken on a pleasant rhythm.

Annie often went to the neighboring towns with Bobby when he sold his wares. They shopped for staples, clothes, and gifts for their Indian friends. On a trip to Cosby, Annie was just coming out of the bank, putting her bankbook into her purse, and not looking where she was going, when she collided with a gentleman, and dropped her purse. He leaned over to pick it up and when he raised his eyes, she was shocked to see that it was her father.

Impulsively, she pulled him to her and gave him a strong hug.

"Daddy," she cried, "I can't believe it. How are you?"

"My little girl," the gruff man was reduced almost to tears. "It is so wonderful to see you again. I never meant what I said that awful day that you left me."

Annie took his arm and started walking with him. "Bobby will be here in a minute. Please wait and see him. Daddy, he makes me very happy. My life in the mountains is wonderful, and we have many friends among the Cherokee."

"I have sorely missed you, Annie. Can we let bygones be bygones? "

"Oh, Daddy, I would be so happy to have you back in my life. "

Bobby showed up then and they shook hands.

J.J. said, "I was wrong. Can you forgive an old man?" He offered his hand to Bobby.

After they shook, Bobby announced, " I'm happy to see you, Sir. I want to invite you to our home. You are always welcome there."

"And you are welcome in mine." J.J. finished the conversation by promising to come up to Cherokee Ridge if Annie and Bobby would first come and have dinner with him in Townsend.

It wasn't very long after that happy meeting, Annie discovered she was going to have a child. Now that she and her father were re-united, the tension she had carried deep within her being which had inhibited her ability to have children, was resolved, and she had three almost in a row.

First they had a son they named Louis, and then, two daughters that they named Lorraine and Annette. When they were old enough, the girls were sent to boarding school in Charleston. When they were grown, Annette took over the J.J.Phillips Fur Trader's store for her grandfather, and Lorraine became a schoolteacher. They never married.

When Robert and Annie were in their fifties the severe winters took their toll on them. They bought a house in Sevierville and left the cabin to Louis, who had also become a trapper. On a visit to his parents, Louis met the neighbor's daughter, Maryann, and they were married in eighteen eighty-nine.

They lived in the cabin with their two children, Rosemarie, and Louis, Junior, whom they called "Sonny". Sonny also became a trapper, outdoing his father in cunning and ability. Rosemarie and Sonny were very close and when she died at a young age he was devastated. When Sonny was eighteen, his parents moved into the house in Sevierville that Robert had left to them.

It wasn't long after that that his life changed.

Sonny Cutter had been warned early in nineteen twenty-seven that he would have to move. He fought the warning by ignoring it. He held out until nineteen thirty-four, long after the Great Smoky Mountains National Park was established.

The land had been taken from the Cherokee Indians, deemed "public lands" and granted to the states of Tennessee and North Carolina. The Agriculture Department had given trusteeship to the National Park Service who took over the tops of the mountains to build the national park.

Sonny wasn't the only objector. There was plenty of public and political opposition, but, eventually, the descendants of the early European pioneers in the area had to relocate. Most of them left peacefully, but Sonny, who had inherited the land the Cherokees had given his Grandfather, and whose family had lived there ever since, resented being evicted and tried to find a place nearest to the old homestead.

He had been a trapper most of his life, like his Daddy and Granddaddy before him. As a young man, he'd brought some pelts down to Townsend where his Aunt Annette introduced him to a pretty woman named Catherine. Her light blonde hair and shy grin reminded him of his sister, Rosemarie, his only playmate of his youth. She had died of complications from the measles when she was twelve and he missed her the rest of his life. That was his first major disappointment. The next was the futility of fighting with the government.

He brought Catherine up to Cherokee Ridge in nineteen twenty-one. She had four stillborn babies before Lou was born, in nineteen thirty-three. She was deathly afraid of losing him, too, so the heart-broken woman gave him only minimal care and no affection in case she would. She shirked her chores, either staying in bed all day, or sitting on the cane rocker on the porch for hours at a time, never speaking. She became a frail shadow of her former self. Sonny tried to bring her out of it until this thing with the national park began.

Frustrated in every direction, the seeds of bitterness grew deep inside of him. He spent most days scouring the area for a place to live, finally deciding to buy a fifty-acre farm near the top of Stonesthrow Ridge, a few miles from Cherokee Ridge. The land was part of an estate of a family who were all now deceased. It had a house, which had been enlarged and improved with plumbing and even an indoor bathroom, but the wear was showing. Sonny hoped Catherine would become enthused enough to fix it up but she just traded one porch seat for another and stayed in her stupor.

The three of them moved in but they each lived there alone. Young Lou knew early on that his Ma wasn't right in the head and he avoided her as much as possible. Sonny taught him to cook and clean, hunt and shoot, as soon as Lou was old enough. Sonny was away alot, sometimes overnight, setting up his "business". It fell to Lou to take care of things at home. Lou grew up ashamed of his mother and terrified of his father.

Sonny was a tall, gaunt man, grim-faced and demanding. He didn't smoke, but he drank the clear white liquid every night that he was home. He had no patience and would often cuff young Lou for no reason. Other times, he would rant and rave about the other residents on Stonesthrow, and how the men all suspected he ran a still but were afraid to confront him.

When Lou was eight years old Catherine caught Pneumonia. She had no strength to fight it and died in her sleep. Sonny told the neighbor's at Baker's store that his wife would be buried in Townsend on her family's plot, and that he and Lou would be over there for a week or two. That kept everyone away from his place while he had her body sent to Townsend and didn't even go to the funeral. Lou never mourned the mother he never had.

From little up, Lou took care of the place as best he could, with school being a welcome respite from his wretched home life. He tried to be friendly with his schoolmates but the tough attitude he'd developed because of his father's ill treatment and bitterness and the secret of his mother's illness turned the other kids away.

He eventually began to think of them as objects of scorn and contempt, and often made sarcastic remarks to them. His

Pa's resentment was passed down to Lou, which made him arrogant. The boys, who were not impressed by his wisecracks, tolerated him. The girls made their dislike obvious or just ignored him. He didn't care about changing until the day he took a liking to little Francie Mann.

School had just started for the day. Lou was coming down the hall when he saw Francie trying to stuff a paper into a book. She dropped the book and Lou went over and swept it up for her.

"Thank you, Lou."

At fifteen, he was tall and lanky. She had to look up. He noticed her eyes were a deep and lovely brown. Her long dark auburn bangs framed her face. Her smile was warm and friendly. In that moment his life changed. He knew he had never seen anything so beautiful.

"I wanted to ask you something." He felt his face getting red and warm. "Can I come over tonight?"

"Why?" She didn't get it.

"To see you," he managed to blurt out before his tongue swelled up and he wouldn't be able to speak again. He started to perspire.

Francie laughed. To him, it was like tiny bells ringing in his head.

"What for?" she asked.

"Because I like you." There! He thought his head was spinning.

"Oh, no." She was surprised. She knew her brothers didn't like him and wouldn't want him there. "I'm sorry, Lou, but I like Hodges Clark."

She went into her classroom and he stood there for a very long moment. He didn't know how to feel. Mortified? Insulted? Hurt? Anger took over. He felt his face get hotter and his fingers clenched until the tips were white.

Embarrassed, he fled the school and ran into the nearby woods. He didn't stop until he reached a little clearing next to the creek. She likes Hodges Clark! He's way too old for her! Maybe when she gets a little older I'll be able to change her mind. His thoughts raced until he saw some sunfish chasing each other in the water. He spent the day there watching them, thinking of Francie and how, someday, they'd be together.

When it was time to go home he returned to the school to get his jacket. He heard Miss Kelly call him. She was a tall, stern lady with too much bluing in her white hair, and wore large eyeglasses, which were attached to a gold chain around her neck. She was usually dressed in a long-sleeved plain black dress with a lacy handkerchief peeking out from beneath one long sleeve. To Lou, she resembled what a prison warden must look like. Her voice was loud and harsh.

"Mr. Cutter." She startled the whole line of students who were just leaving. No one wanted Miss Kelly's wrath.

Lou looked around but Francie, Ada and Georgie were nowhere in sight. Thank goodness! They must have gone before he got back. He swaggered over to the teacher, a tough grin on his face, trying to disguise his apprehension. He looked puny next to her in spite of his advanced height for his age.

"Here's a note for your Father. See that he gets it." She thrust the note into his sweaty hand.

He walked home slowly, so as not to meet up with the rest of the kids. He felt flushed and frustrated. He hoped Francie wouldn't tell anyone what happened. Unknown to him, Francie had forgotten the incident right after it happened, and, on the way home, she, Ada and Georgie were comparing notes on their homework.

Lou hoped his Pa wouldn't be home when he got there. He didn't see him right away. Sonny was working on the door lock of his 1941 Oldsmobile sedan. The body had some dents and dings but he kept the engine in tip-top condition.

When Lou came in the driveway with the note still sticking out of his hand, "What've you got there, Boy?" Sonny called, as he stood up behind the car.

He took the note Lou reluctantly held out to him and read it.

"You stupid kid!" Sonny slapped him so hard on the side of the head he could feel his lip bleeding.

"I don't care what you do. You'd just better not get caught. I don't need the law snooping around here." He hit him again, knocking him to the ground.

"Get in and clean up. We're going up the ridge tonight. I think it's time I teach you the family business."

Lou got up slowly and tried to wipe the blood off his face with his knuckles. It was a good day when Sonny didn't hit him for some reason. He went inside, washed up and prepared supper. His lip had a slight cut on it but his jaw didn't swell.

When they had eaten, Lou cleaned up the kitchen and went out on the porch. Sonny was waiting for him. He picked up a heavy walking stick he had carved long ago and with Lou trailing in his footsteps, he pounded the ground as they climbed trying to scare off any rattlesnakes that might be about.

The route they took was so circuitous, Lou thought he could never find the site again by himself. Up near the top of their ridge, there was a still. There were two men there.

"This is my kid." Sonny got right to work.

Lou noticed that Sonny's eyes were cold and hard. He paid close attention. He knew Sonny expected him to know after being told just once.

Sonny picked up a pewter dish from atop a crate. He opened a container that had "Gunpowder" written on the side and spooned some of the black powder onto the dish. Then he ladled some alcohol from the tub at the end of the still onto the black powder and ignited it with a cigarette lighter.

"That's fine," he nodded to the two men. He explained to Lou, "That is what is known as proving the alcohol. This'll be your job for a while until I can teach you more. If it doesn't ignite, it's been watered down and you must check the bead, which are the bubbles that form on top of the liquid. The more bead it has, the more alcohol will be in it. We want it 100% proof, or 50% alcohol."

"If we leave you here after you know the routine and you hear a loud bird whistle, douse the fire and scat up on the ridge and hide. Now, after you've proven the pot liquor you can rinse those jars in the creek. That'll be enough for your first lesson."

Spring Break found Lou learning all about moonshine: to use warm water to ferment the mash, and watch the process carefully until it finished fermenting; to fill the boiler about three-quarters full to give the liquid room to foam; to add cold water into the cooling tub as the vapor in the coil emptied into the tub and the water ran out of the bottom; to control the temperature so the liquid didn't gush out.

Sonny showed him how to see if a drop of "shine" on his fingers felt greased, and to collect a few drops on the back of a spoon to make sure it smelled correctly.

Most importantly, he was taught to discard the first few jars so the methanol wouldn't poison anyone. He learned all there was to know as soon as he could, rather than face his Daddy's anger again.

When school reopened, Lou avoided the rest of his schoolmates more than ever. The few who noticed were relieved not to have to put up with his wisecracks and gladly left him alone. He especially avoided Francie but she was on his mind day and night. He daydreamed that one day he and Francie would get married and his terrible life would be transformed. For the time being, though, he had to please his Pa.

* * *

That summer, Lou's days consisted of helping with the moonshine business and tending to his regular chores, but he was almost happy when Sonny decided to teach him to drive. He knew Sonny kept that old car in A-one condition and now, he could understand why. That was their delivery vehicle.

Lou was an apt pupil. Driving gave him a feeling of exhilaration he had never known. For the first time in his life he developed an air of self-confidence.

When he turned sixteen Sonny let him quit school. He became an experienced driver, practicing on the gravel roads and forest trails high above the ridges, and on steep, winding roads and narrow passages parallel to the main road up the mountain, towards North Carolina, past great rock outcroppings and cascading streams.

A few peaks were over five thousand feet, with isolated valleys, where some of their customers lived. Sonny delivered large quantities, frequently, in the summer, since it was impossible to get over the mountains in the winter and the spring thaws brought muddy road ruts and impassable driving conditions.

The night after his sixteenth birthday, Lou was up at the still by himself. Night birds were beginning to call. He gazed at the rippling water as the stream curved down from the mountaintops, softly gurgling as it passed, not giving a hint of the tempest it would become when it joined other branches further down the mountain, swelling into the Little Pigeon River, which coursed through the valley below.

Like his pa before him, Lou Cutter loved and breathed the Smoky Mountains. He knew what Cherokee Ridge had meant to his ancestors and his pa, and he realized that Stonesthrow was just as important to him. He'd never want to think about leaving.

He thought of Francie. Once in awhile, he'd see her as he passed the Mann farm on the way to Bubba's store. She was thirteen, now, and getting prettier every day. One day, when she is grown, he believed, we'll be married and be happy up here on the mountain. "That's all I'll ever need," he told himself, "Francie and Stonesthrow."

Sonny had parked the car high upon the ridge in an overgrown field where it would be unseen by either hikers or airplanes. He told Lou there was a large delivery to be made just over the state line and he wanted him to go there alone for the first time.

Lou carried the crate of jars up to the car and went back for the second one. At that time, Rich Morris, Sonny's partner and his helper, Jimmie Blake, showed up to tend the still.

Lou was excited. "Glad to see you, Men. I have to go over the mountain."

Rich, another squinty-eyed, mean-looking mountain man like Sonny, chuckled, "Be careful of those loose women over there."

Lou had no idea what he meant, but he chuckled, too.

Rich continued, "Your pa said he'd be up here in a bit."

"I'm sorry I won't be here to help."

"We'll be fine. All we need are two men and a taster," he laughed, as he recited the moonshiner's creed.

Lou went back up the ridge and drove off. The moon was slowly climbing over the mountain as he traveled. When he went with Sonny the deliveries were always received by Pa Walker, in full company of his four grown sons, all tight-lipped, stone-faced mountaineers, who hurriedly emptied the trunk of the car without saying a word. Lou felt very grown-up until he thought about the Walker men.

They made their living hunting and trapping, selling the pelts, and the snakeskin belts and hatbands they fashioned from their quarry. Lou always felt he and Sonny couldn't leave fast enough. He was afraid, this time, he might provoke them in some way. As much as he enjoyed driving, the Walker place was one place he dreaded going to. Lou didn't know whom he was more afraid of, his Pa or the Walker men.

The last part of the route was an old logging trail, lumpy and bumpy. Lou knew he had to go slowly so as not to have any of the jars break. When he arrived at the Walker's he jumped out of the car and opened the trunk. Everything was all right. He realized the Walker sons were not standing there ready to empty his cargo. He looked around

He saw a woman come out of the house. In the bright moonlight he could see that she was young and lovely. She had long, dark brown hair, a curvaceous body and when she smiled at him, the whitest teeth he had ever seen.

"Hey!"

He had never heard such a velvety voice before.

"Daddy and the boys are trapping. They won't be home until tomorrow. Come and sit up here with me awhile."

He lifted a crate of jars, carried them up the three steps and set them down near the upright that held the porch roof up. He went back down the steps and brought the other crate up. When he was finished he sat on the top step next to her. She was wearing an off the shoulder white ruffled blouse and a long full skirt which covered her legs as she sat, revealing only her painted toenails.

He felt a sense of excitement that was new to him. He could smell a flowery perfume in the air.

"What's your name, Boy?" There was that velvet sound again.

"Lou, Ma'am." He felt as though his voice had no volume.

"How old are you?" She smiled, and threw her head back and laughed.

"I'm sixteen, Ma'am." Lou wondered what was so funny

"Ma'am! I'll show you who's an old ma'am. Come in here."

She stood up, taking his hand as he stood, too. She ushered him into an alcove off the kitchen, divided from the rest of the room only by a flimsy curtain. "I'm just eighteen. I ain't no old ma'am!" She smiled that wonderful smile again.

That night, she taught him what life was all about. She told him her name was Charlotte, but she was called Lottie. He discovered that he really didn't mind driving to the Walker's place, anymore. He went with wild anticipation and when her father and brothers weren't home, Lottie treated him very well.

He still had plans that he would marry Francie someday, but in his boyish mind he loved Lottie, too. That came in handy when, one day in late October, just before the first heavy winter storm, five angry men showed up at the Cutter's door, shotguns in hand, lowered to their knees, but at the ready.

Lou knew Sonny would always be a force to reckon with when he said, "Is this true, Lou?

"Yes, Pa." Lou was frantic. He didn't know whom he was more afraid of.

"Well, then, bring her here and he'll marry her. " Sonny settled the matter right there.

The men were satisfied with that and the next day, Lottie Walker married Lou Cutter and moved in with him and his pa. The first son was born in the late Spring. They called him Junior. Two more boys followed, Billy and Jack.

Charlotte, the loving temptress, the femme fatale of the mountains, may have been an exceptional lover, but as a mother she was a failure. The babies only got the minimum care she had to exert and were on their own as soon as they could walk and talk, running barefoot in the summer and getting into mischief. She avoided Sonny as much as she could. She resented his apparent hold on Lou and felt that Lou would always defer to his pa. Eventually, she blamed Lou for trapping her into this forlorn existence.

Lou tried to appease her for a few years, remodeling some of the house, adding another bathroom upstairs, letting her buy fancy clothes in Gatlinburg, even taking her and the boys to the annual neighborhood picnics, until it became sharply evident that the other wives on the mountain found nothing in common with her and she stopped going.

"Did you wash the grapes well?" Mrs. Mann automatically sifted the grapes in the colander. "I washed the jars this morning while you were in school."

"Yes, Ma'am." Francie enjoyed making jelly. She had helped her mother do it for so long she now was able to do it herself. Tomorrow night, she had plans to make blueberry jam. She poured the washed grapes into the stockpot and mashed them with the back of the wooden spoon.

"Mama, guess what Ada told me?"

"What's that, Francie?" her mother lined the gleaming jars up on the counter.

"She said that her mother has met a man in Gatlinburg and they seem to be serious. They may get married."

"Who is he?" Mrs. Mann took over stirring the grapes as Francie left the stove to get a drink of water.

"He's a real estate agent who rented her the store she took to sell her items to the tourists. I think his name is 'von Schlammer'. I don't know if Ada told me his first name. She says he's a real snappy dresser. He usually wears a suit with a vest, with a pocket watch and a fob, a bowler hat, and even a walking stick, and looks real fine. She's met him a few times and he always dresses like that."

"I remember when she began renting that store." Mrs. Mann remarked. "Honey, you'd better pin up your hair. Marie had made too many woven blankets and rugs and needed her own place to sell them, rather than selling them to another business. She is a hard worker, that Marie Wightman."

Francie hurried into the bedroom, grabbed a barrette and tried to pin up her long, unruly hair. She was back in an instant.

"Ada says the wedding will be in one of those chapels in Gatlinburg and we would all be invited. Have you ever been to Gatlinburg, Mama?"

"Yes. It's quite a place. Like a carnival that never goes home, I'd say. Lots to see and do." Her mother strained the grapes as she spoke, then poured the juice in bowl.

"You'll need a new dress. I probably will, too." Mrs. Mann spoke, absent-mindedly. She was thinking of Marie And Ada. They didn't have it easy, but Marie kept things together with creativity, talent and hard work. She was admired by all of the neighbors.

The jelly was put into the jars and left to be covered.

Francie sat down at the table. "I hope I can have a big wedding when I get married."

Her mother smiled. "Who will you marry, Francie?"

Francie blushed. "Mama, I would like to marry Hodges when I'm older. He always helps everyone, and he's so thoughtful in so many ways."

Her mother sat opposite her and smiled, "Hodges is another hard worker. I think he might be a little old for you, what do you think? You have plenty of time."

"No, Mama, I think he's just the right age." Francie got up and put the lids on the jars. "Tomorrow, I am giving Hodges a jar for his family."

"That'll be nice. Now, you'd better go to bed. You have school tomorrow. Good night, Sweetheart. "

They gave each other a peck on the cheek and Francie went to her room while her mother sat in the living room and waited for her husband who had gone to a meeting at church with the boys. She couldn't wait for him to get home to tell him what Francie had said.

When Ralph and Billy came in with their dad they stopped in the kitchen to pick up a cupcake and went right to their rooms. Frank came and sat with his wife.

"We decided the parish house needed fresh paint in the party room so we're all going to paint it on Saturday. Would you be up to making a casserole for us? Your hot turkey salad would go over big." He threw his arm around her on the couch and rubbed her shoulder as he spoke.

"Of course" she said. "Will Ralph and Billy help?"

"Yes, and I was surprised that they agreed. I had a feeling they'd be busy studying or something."

They both laughed. The boys were notorious about only working when a payday was included.

"Well, Francie said that Ada told her her mom is going to be married. To the real estate man who rented her that store she has in Gatlinburg."

"I know who you mean. He's a really nice man. Dresses a bit extremely but he can get away with it. Even has a walking stick. The guys were talking about him at Bubba's. They were in last week for a minute, he and Marie. She introduced us but never mentioned marriage."

"I guess it was a recent idea. Francie wants to go to the wedding. We'll each need a new dress." Mrs. Mann yawned and said, "I'm tired. It's been a long day."

Mr. Mann put out the lamp and they went to bed.

The next day at school Ada told Francie it was settled. Her mother and her stepfather-to-be planned to get married Christmas Eve, at a chapel in Gatlinburg. They will stay on Stonesthrow until Ada gets married, and, after that, at his apartment in town during the week, and Marie's house on Stonesthrow on weekends. Mrs. Wightman had insisted on that because she loved being on the mountain. Said it gave her respite from the crowds of tourists, plus, it also lets her gather her herbs and flowers for her crafts. She said Vonnie was totally agreeable.

Francie said," I just hope the roads are okay and there isn't any snow. I can't wait to go there. I have never seen a wedding, and I've never been to Gatlinburg. My mom says it is beautiful."

Ada replied, "I've gone to her store there with her, and it really is a nice place. I will be the maid of honor and she's asked Bubba to give her away. Mr. von Schlammer, I call him Vonnie, is from Germany, and since he has no relatives here, he asked Mr. Brinks to be his best man."

"Isn't it all too exciting?" Francie was getting more and more interested in the whole idea. "When will you and Georgie get married?"

"After graduation. That's two more years. Of course, Georgie would marry tomorrow if they'd let him, but he realizes we need our education." Ada laughed.

"Mom and I were making jelly last night and I told her I want to marry Hodges."

"What did she say?" Ada wasn't surprised. She knew Francie had had a crush on Hodges since she was old enough to think about having a boyfriend.

"She said I had plenty of time." Francie answered. "Anyway, he's never asked me." She giggled, and said, "I do have plenty of time. After all, I'm almost fifteen. I guess I'd better think about graduating first, too."

They had gone to the lunchroom and joined Georgie for lunch.

"Are you going to help paint the parish house? My brothers are even going, and my mom is cooking." Francie opened her lunch bag and gave Ada and Georgie each a jar of jelly.

"Thanks," Georgie put the jelly in his bag and began eating his lunch.

Ada said, "Georgie, I'll come over, too. That way, I can help with the food. I'll bake some Brownies."

"Great," he always seemed to agree with whatever Ada said.

Francie watched this with fascination. "I only hope I am as lucky in love as you are, Ada."

"Oh, Francie, I know you will be."

After lunch, they went back to class and the rest of the day went by quickly.

A slow drizzle had begun by the time they left school. As they came out the side door they heard a horn blow. It was Hodges Clark, in his old Dodge.

"Hi," he called. "Come on, Francie, Ada, George. I was down in the valley and on my way home, so I thought I'd stop and pick you up because of the rain." He had a big grin on his face.

They ran, laughing, and jumped in the car.

"What a break. Thanks, Hodge," Georgie said. He added, "You can drop me off at Ada's. Appreciate it."

"Sure." Hodges turned out of the school parking lot.

After he dropped Ada and Georgie off at Ada's, Hodges headed back up the road towards home. Francie asked, "Will you be at the church on Saturday? It sounds as if everyone will be there."

"I'm supplying the paint." Hodges laughed. He glanced over at her as he drove around the curves. She was so cute. He remembered the time her father wanted to have his wheat combined and she was ready to work just as hard as anyone else, and she couldn't have been more than twelve. Mr. Mann had asked Brinksy to bring the combine over, only to find that the wheat wasn't high enough to reach the machine.

"Do you remember the time your dad had Mr. Brinks come over to combine the wheat field?"

Francie laughed. "I sure do. My dad always wanted to farm completely organically, so he didn't add fertilizer. Therefore, the wheat didn't grow tall enough to combine. That was so funny. Oh, Hodges, here's some jelly for you and your folks." She took a jar from her lunch bag and propped it up on the car seat next to him.

"Thanks, Francie. Yes, and we were all out in the wheat field picking it by hand. Your dad is so much fun. I always enjoy it when he calls me to help with something or other. He has such a good sense of humor and makes everything so enjoyable. It's not work when we work with him."

"That's not the half of it Hodges. Remember the time he took the bus to Oklahoma to visit my grandma?"

"That was last year, wasn't it? It was during the Spring rains when the roads were too muddy to drive through."

"Yes. He told the lady at the bank he was going to Oklahoma in a fifty thousand dollar Lincoln with a chauffeur.

The lady seemed shocked, until she finally said, 'Why are you farming on Stonesthrow, then, if you have a fifty thousand dollar Lincoln and a chauffer?' Hodges, he was talking about the bus!"

They had just reached the Mann farm, when she finished telling him the story and he was laughing loud and long as she got out of the car.

"Thanks for the ride," she called, as she ran to the house.

Hodges watched her go, thinking how fond he was of Francie. He realized that someday, he'd ask her to marry him.

The only people on Stonesthrow who didn't go to the wedding were the Cutter's, since Lottie had just had her second baby and wasn't feeling up to it.

Bubba closed the store because he was giving Marie away. He always liked Marie. He had sold her his house across the highway, and at first had wondered how a widow could possibly live way up there in the mountains and get along, especially with a little girl. When he saw what she could do with her crafts, he was filled with admiration and was proud to help her whenever he could. He wasn't surprised when she brought her beau to the store. Marie would have made a good catch for anyone, he thought. Although this gentleman was a bit older than she, Bubba felt they were well suited to each other.

The chapel was small and the neighbors on the mountain filled all the pews. Marie had made matching dresses for herself and Ada, of ice blue satin. They had dried wildflowers twined around ribbon hanging all through their hair, and bouquets of dried flowers made their outfits complete. It was hard to tell who was the most beautiful.

Francie and her mother had shopped at a little place in Cosby where they usually bought Francie's school clothes. When she heard it was for a wedding the shopkeeper sent to Knoxville for special evening dresses they had picked out of her catalog. Francie's was silver gray overlay with a pink slip beneath. The dress shimmered in the light whenever she moved and made a soft rustling sound. Lily Mann's dress was fuchsia satin, had a high neck and long sleeves, with sequins around the neckline and cuffs of the sleeves. Francie wore pink ribbons in her hair, while her mother wore a tiny pillbox hat which matched the gray winter coat she wore.

Marybelle, Evelyn, and Evelyn's daughter, Madeleine, who had come over from Knoxville to watch her father be best man, enjoyed the excuse to dress up, and they all looked lovely. Mrs. Crewe and Carol stayed at Marie's to fix the late supper they were all having when they returned.

The wedding brought a tear to many an eye in the small chapel and when it was over they all drove back to the Wightman home on Stonesthrow for a late supper and punch. Georgie and Ada agreed they wanted their wedding to be just like it. Hodges came over to Francie and told her how beautiful she looked, and she blushed. He laughed, and he saw that she was embarrassed.

"Don't mind me, Francie," he whispered. "I just had to tell you how pretty you look tonight. I'm sorry for laughing." He sat down next to her and asked her if she wanted some punch.

"No, thanks, Hodges. I'm afraid I'd spill it on my dress. Billy's here." She jumped up and ran to the front hallway. Her brother Billy, always the aspiring musician, had promised to bring up a small group of friends to play at the party. He was alone.

"Where is the rest of the band?" Francie asked, as she helped him with his parka.

"They each had gigs in Gatlinburg. Merry Christmas, everybody," Billy called to the room full of people as he went near the window by the sofa to set up his guitar.

"In that case," Brinksy laughed, "I'm glad I brought my fiddle. I'll go get it. Didn't want to horn in on your band, Bill, but since they're not here, I'll play with you, if that's okay."

"That'll be great, Mr. Brinks. By the way, you sure look spiffy tonight."

Tom Brinks winked to the roomful of friends as he said, "That's because I am the best man."

Everyone laughed, as Evelyn waved her hand at him, as if to say, "go away."

The party went on until midnight, with chili and cornbread, eggnog and punch, and a huge wedding cake that Mr.von Schlammer had brought earlier from the bakery in Gatlinburg. Bubba made a toast to the new couple and everyone laughed when he finished by saying, "May all your troubles be little ones." Ada and Francie had no idea what was so funny.

By now, it was Christmas day and everyone wanted to get home and get some sleep before what would traditionally be a busy day at each home. They all wished Marie and her new husband well and said goodnight. It had begun snowing softly, and they were all happy it had waited until they were safely home.

Billy went to the Crewe's to visit with Carol for a little while, and Georgie, who said goodnight to Ada, promised to see her later in the day.

When the Mann's arrived home, Francie hated to put on her nightgown. She was still very excited.

"Mama, thank you so much for this beautiful dress. She rustled the fabric this way and that, loving the sound it made. "I think I will put it away and wear it when I get married."

Mrs. Mann laughed, "I think, by then, Francie, we'll be able to buy you a nice, new dress. In the meantime, you can wear it to church now and then. Goodnight."

It was now nineteen fifty-three and the annual neighborhood picnic was held at the Keene's. It was a sunny day, not too hot or humid. The potluck dinner had included some incredibly delicious food. The men played horseshoes while the women chatted and shared recipes and quilting patterns. Everyone on Stonesthrow was there except for Lou and Lottie Cutter, who were expecting their third child any day.

After playing the winner, who was usually Bubba Baker, Hodges went over to the food table to get cold lemonade. Francie was sitting next to her mother, looking just as sad as could be. Hodges walked back to the game, wondering what could be wrong.

Just then, Bubba lost, for the first time that day, and after everyone cheered for his good games, the men all sat down near the women.

Frank Mann stood up. "May I have your attention, please?"

"So formal," Bubba laughed, as he sat beside Evelyn Brinks, and wiped his sweaty brow.

"As you all know," he went on, "our Ralph has joined the Navy. Bill now lives in the valley."

They all tried not to stare at Carol Crewe who was there with her boyfriend, Bud. Bud was an appliance repairman who had come up to the Crewe's to set up their new washing machine. Carol, who dated Billy through high school, was smitten, and now she and Bud were talking about getting married. Mrs. Crewe smiled at Frank.

"What's Billy up to these days, Frank?" Marybelle asked.

"He works at the Victory Bakery down there. On the weekends, he plays guitar with a country music group and is trying to start a band of his own.

"What I do want to let you all know is this. My brother in Oklahoma writes that our mother isn't doing too well. He's offered me a job as a salesman in his tractor business there and so we will be leaving Stonesthrow. Not that we won't miss it. It's the only home the kids have ever known, but with the boys away, we'll just have Francie and we plan to try to make her just as happy there as she's been here."

The news stunned everyone. The Mann's had been on Stonesthrow since their marriage years ago. They were well liked and admired, and everyone at the picnic felt a sense of loss.

They all had a million questions, except Hodges, who went into the house on the pretense of refilling the lemonade pitcher. He couldn't believe it. Overwhelmed with disappointment, he waited in the kitchen, trying to control his emotions. How could he lose Francie? He had loved her since she was a young girl. She couldn't be going so far away. He couldn't let her.

Somehow, he muddled through the rest of the afternoon and when it was time to leave, he and Francie walked home, hand in hand, neither saying very much. He made plans to come by her house that evening, still trying to decide what to do.

Francie had no idea what was in the back of his mind, but she was very upset about leaving Stonesthrow. She agreed to meet him at her 'bacca barn after supper and see if they could arrange some way out of this mess.

Francie was almost sixteen and had known Hodges Clark all of her life. She knew he had a kind and gentle way, but that he could be firm and decisive when it was necessary. He loved the mountains as she did, and had never wanted to be anything other than a farmer. He looked so young and vulnerable in the twilight she leaned over and kissed him softly. He began to speak.

"Francie, I've been thinking about it since your father first spoke of leaving. I can't let you go so far away. I have loved you since you were a little girl and I was waiting to tell you when you got a little older. I know we can make it if you will marry me."

She had tears in her eyes. "Oh, Hodges, I have always loved you, too. I want to marry you but Daddy will never let me until I'm older. And I'll go to Oklahoma and I'll never see you again. Or Stonesthrow."

"No, I have it all figured out. We'll elope."

Hodges Clark grew up in a family of women. His four older sisters doted on him, but they insisted he learn mountain ways. He logged, plowed, planted, reaped, and raised livestock, all with their support and encouragement. He became a partner to Stonesthrow, toughing out the harsh Winters, planting in the glorious Springs, working tobacco, and logging, through the busy Summers, and praising the harvest in the Fall, when the spectacular colors of the foliage filled him with a sense of awe and contentment. Well-muscled, tall, lean and fit at twenty-one, he had loved Francie since she was a little girl.

Francie Mann knew no other home. She took living on Stonesthrow for granted, enjoying sledding in the Winter, tossing rocks at planting time, helping with the Summer canning and preserving, and gathering the brightly colored leaves in the Fall to press in one of her many scrapbooks, but she wasn't aware of how much she loved the mountains until her father decided to move to Oklahoma.

It was incomprehensible to Francie to leave Stonesthrow. Nowhere on earth could be as fulfilling. Nowhere else could ever be Home. Leaving Hodges Clark was just as impossible. Their lives had always been intertwined. She prayed often for a miracle, and knew her prayers had been answered when Hodges proposed.

She wanted to tell her mother and Ada, and she had a bittersweet happiness about the wedding. Always a practical girl, Francie decided it would be best not to say anything at this time. She went to sleep with a delicious secret, realizing that, tomorrow night, one of her long-time dreams would come true—she would be Mrs. Hodges Clark.

Hodges, on the other hand, spent the night hoping he was doing the right thing. His good conscience told him that Francie was very young. But, his other side argued, mountain folks usually marry young. Her folks won't be around. But mine will. And I'll always take good care of her. She loves

Stonesthrow as much as I do. And I love her more than anything, even the mountain.

The next day, he drove right past the cutoff to the main highway and on to the road toward Sevierville.

"I've never been this far before," she stated, as he drove over the Little Pigeon River bridge. It was a high span, over three quarters of a mile long. "Wow!" she exclaimed, looking down at the rocky river bed below. "That's a long way down."

"Yes." he agreed. "And it's shallow, there, too." He was going to add that a fall from that height would mean certain death but he didn't want to take her mind off the happy occasion this was supposed to be so he just added that they only had a few more miles to go.

It took them about an hour and a half before he pulled up at a large gray house with white trim. There was a sign hanging on a metal post reading Justice of the Peace. Hodges went up the steps and rang the bell. A plump, white-haired woman in a blue housedress opened the door.

"We want to get married." Hodges sounded so confident. Francie hung back as the lady eyed her up and down.

"Do you have a license?"

"Well, no." Hodges stammered for the first time.

"Well, you need one." The lady thought to herself, these mountain kids get younger every year. She noticed they were trying very hard to appear grown-up, and her heart went out to them. "The Judge won't be here until four p.m., anyway, so you have time to go to the courthouse to get one. The courthouse is two blocks over, on Court Street. "They turned to leave as she called after them, "You'll need a witness."

Francie stopped for a second but Hodges took her hand and pulled her along as he whispered, "I know someone."

She was concerned, but when they got back into the car he told her that his Great-Aunt Blanche lived nearby and that she'd stand up for them.

"But, Hodges, she doesn't know me." Francie was disappointed.

Hodges reassured her. "It's okay. Wait until you meet her. She's my Pa's aunt, and she's really nice. She used to be a music teacher. Uncle Howard died in the war and was buried at Normandy. She never remarried. She's always been a real sweetheart."

He drove down a tree lined side street and stopped in front of a row of two family homes. He parked and helped Francie out of the car. They walked up the sidewalk to the door of number thirty-four and he rang the bell. Almost immediately, he door opened and a chubby, gray-haired, jolly lady grabbed Hodges and gave him a bear hug.

"Why, Hodges Clark, what brings you to Sevierville? And to see your old Aunt Blanche. Why, it's been a time, hasn't it? I haven't seen you since your graduation. Come on in." She opened the door further and reached behind him, taking Francie gently by the arm. "You, too, Honey."

She guided them into a lovely, neat living room and motioned for them to sit on the couch. She sat in a wooden chair, opposite.

"Boy," she started. Her voice was melodious, and Francie thought she must be a wonderful singer. Everything about her, the room, the furniture, and even herself, was bright and cheerful and Francie took an immediate liking to her.

"This chair sets good," Aunt Blanche said, as she lovingly rubbed the wooden arms. "We got this as a wedding present when we lived up on the mountain with your folks. If someone offered me a million dollars, I couldn't say who made it for us."

She leaned over to Francie. "That was the custom way back then, did you know?"

Without waiting for an answer she went on. "When a couple married the neighbors all gave the woman a household item and either built a piece of furniture or gave the man a farm implement. Those were the days. Do they still do that?"

Again, she didn't wait for an answer but continued, "Goodness Me! I'm going on and on, and haven't even asked why you're here. It must be something important. Please forgive me, Honey." She gave Francie a broad, kind smile. "I'm three months behind in my talking."

Francie smiled back.

Hodges said, "We've come to be married, Aunt B, and we need a witness to get the license. Would you come with us to get it?"

"Well," she slapped the arm of the chair. "I'd be honored to help my favorite nephew." She practically shooed them out of the house as she stopped at the hall tree, picked up her purse, plopped her hat on her head and straightened her collar. "Let's get going."

They drove to the courthouse and found the license bureau. Aunt Blanche, with a twinkle in her warm, brown eyes, raised her right hand and told the court clerk that she had known Francie since she was a baby and that Hodges was her nephew. The youngsters were a little nervous but the clerk signed the papers and gave the license to Hodges.

When they got back outside, Hodges asked Aunt Blanche if she wanted to go get an ice cream soda since they had time until the judge returned. Too late, he realized he'd used the extra money he had with him to get the license, and he needed the rest to pay the Judge.

Aunt Blanche came to the rescue once again. "Let me treat you kids. That'll be an early wedding present. I'll send you something really nice when you get home."

After they had the ice cream sodas, Hodges dropped her off at her house. "Are you sure you don't want to come with us?"

"No thank you, Darling. I have to go to a meeting at church. They are voting on a new parish house and I'm on the committee." She hugged them both and laughed. "Next time you get to town be sure to come and see me."

Francie thanked her and got back in the car. Hodges gave her a hug and a kiss and watched as she went back into the house.

They returned to the Judge's place. When the lady opened the door this time, Hodges waved the paper at her. "We're here and we're ready."

She ushered them into a tiny study. The walls were lined with dark wooden bookshelves filled with books. The upright chairs were harder than church pews. Hodges squirmed. He talked out of the side of his mouth in case the lady was nearby. "I hope we don't have to wait too long."

At this, Francie began to giggle. Soon, everything he said was funny and she tried to stifle it but she just kept giggling until the door opened and an elderly man bounded into the room so quickly she thought he might bump into the opposite wall. This caught her trying to quell even more giggles.

He had snow white frizzy hair, surrounding a bald spot, overgrown eyebrows, where some hairs stood straight up while others lay in various directions on his forehead, bifocals which hung halfway down his nose and an air of friendliness, in spite of his powerful position.

They both stood up and Hodges gripped her hand, as if to tell her to stop giggling. She cleared her throat the same time as the judge did, which made her almost laugh out loud. Finally, she cleared it again and stood up taller, trying to act like a lady as her mother had always admonished her.

The ceremony was short and direct, although to Francie, it seemed endless. She just wanted it to be over, because she had visions of her mother and father rushing to Sevierville on the warpath, punishing them both. Then the judge was saying, "You may kiss the bride."

Francie caught sight of the Judge's benevolent smile as Hodges took her in his arms and gave her her first real kiss.

She almost swooned, but she could feel Hodges' strong muscular arms holding her tight, keeping it all together.

When Hodges and Francie arrived back on Stonesthrow and announced they had been married, Mr. Mann scared them both as he raised his hand, made a fist and started to shoot it out toward Hodges' face. Before he connected, he grinned a big grin and shook Hodges hand, instead.

"Congratulations! I couldn't have wanted a better man for my little girl."

Mrs. Mann hugged Francie and then, Hodges. "How did you get the license?"

"Oh, Mama." Francie was laughing and crying at the same time. "Hodges' Aunt Blanche came with us. She's such a nice lady. Are you sure you're happy?"

Her Mother led her over to the kitchen table and they sat.

"I am sorry that you didn't tell us first, but I guess because you're so young we probably would have asked you to wait. Now, how about something to celebrate." She got up and fixed four glasses of iced tea. She put some homemade cookies on a plate and they all sat together.

Mr. Mann said, "Now, I have to think up a really good wedding gift for you two."

Hodges said, "All we need is your blessing, Sir."

"We can do more than that." Mr. Mann smiled as he realized he had just the gift. "Since we are getting ready to move to Oklahoma, we were going to sell the farm but we've decided to divide the land between Francie, Ralph and Billy. We are deeding you the ridge adjoining your land. You will have plenty of timber to log, enough to keep you into your old age."

Francie and Hodges couldn't believe their ears. Hodges had told her they'd live with his parents for a while. Since his four sisters were all grown and gone there'd be plenty of room until he could build a cabin for them on the ridge across the creek. Now, they'd have their own piece of Heaven some day, and on their own land.

After they left the Mann's they went to the Clark's. Lem and Lucy were overjoyed that they had the daughter-in-law they'd always hoped for, and that Stonesthrow would keep its own.

It was a sunny afternoon, and Lou was returning from Newport where he'd gone to buy some more mason jars. As he passed Bubba's store, Tom Brinks came running out and flagged him down.

"What is it?" Lou was in a good mood and his remark seemed friendly to Tom.

"My tractor is in need of a repair, Lou. It just quit on me over to the Wightman's place. I was mowing her back forty. I had to leave it there. Will you be free to stop over tomorrow and check it out for me? I have no idea what it could be."

Tom didn't like Lou or his pa but Lou was a crackerjack mechanic. Little did anyone except Sonny know that he got all of his expertise from keeping the "delivery" car, running.

"I think I'll be free after lunch." Lou laughed to himself. He was self-employed and could do anything he wanted.

Tom had no idea what Lou was thinking. He just saw the big smile Lou gave him. Tom leaned on the driver's side door and added, "Oh, did you know? Francie Mann and Hodges Clark were married yesterday? They eloped."

Lou felt the blood rush to his head. The smile disappeared and he tried to hide his shock. "No kidding!" He couldn't think of anything to say. His mouth got very dry.

Tom went on. "They will live with the Clark's for awhile. What a cute couple. I do believe they were in love since they were kids." Tom had no idea what the news was doing to Lou.

Lou's demeanor changed immediately. "Well, I gotta get

home, now." He floored the truck, almost driving over Tom's foot.

"See you tomorrow?" Tom called after him, wondering what changed Lou so quickly. He watched Lou drive, thinking that he was going faster than he should on this road, before he went back into Bubba's.

All the way home and late into the night, Lou couldn't get used to the idea that Hodges had eloped with Francie. He felt that Hodges had stolen what should have been his girl. He was surly to Lottie, who was about to have their third son, any day.

"What's up with you?" Lottie was grouchy today. It had been a difficult pregnancy and the warm weather didn't help.

"Nothing." Lou barked. "No supper, again?"

"I didn't feel like it." She seldom fixed supper for Lou and Sonny, usually eating with the babies.

Lou stormed out again. Lottie had begun arguing a lot, lately, and he wasn't in the mood to spar with her. He had to think things through. Francie and Hodges. He couldn't get over it. She's too young to be married, he thought, as he climbed the ridge toward the still. He was getting angrier by the minute.

Sonny was there, along with his buddy, Rich Morris.

"Where's Jimmie?" Lou masked his feelings in front of his pa. Jimmie Blake, a slow-witted young man about twenty years old, usually came over from Hidden Hollow with Rich, whom Sonny had known when he was a trapper on Cherokee Ridge. The boy didn't have an original thought in his head but did what he was told. He was delighted to receive a few dollars and all the white lightening he wanted in return for helping with a few of the more mundane chores at the still.

"He's down with the Flu." Rich shrugged, as he poured the fermented mash into the boiler. He was a good friend to Sonny but Lou felt outnumbered by the two former mountain men. He studied the scrawny man with the thinning gray hair as Rich chewed on a plug of tobacco and spit the saliva away from the mixture in the kettle. Lou knew that Rich may be a stringbean of a man but there was never a doubt in his mind this former trapper possessed a mighty strength that could be uncompromising. He always tried to stay on Rich's good side.

"Then, I guess it's good I came up." Lou put some cold water into the cooling tub as he spoke. Sonny knew something was wrong.

"Is she on you, again?" He had hated Lottie from day one, feeling that she had trapped Lou into marriage. He saw that she was not a good mother, either, doing as little as she possibly had to for the babies. It didn't phase him. He had raised Lou single-handedly and he would help Lou raise the boys and the new child. In his mind, they needed no one else. It had always just been the two of them, and that had been fine for Sonny.

"Nah! Pa, did you know Hodges Clark eloped with the Mann girl?"

"Well, ain't that just fine?" Sonny sneered. "Ol' Lem's got his self a new doll, huh? Now that all his are grown and gone, I guess they needed some young blood." His eyes flashed, viciously, and he smirked at Rich, who laughed at the nasty implication.

Lou had never told his pa how he felt about Francie all these years. He wanted to defend her, but kept silent. His anger grew to the boiling point.

"I'm going home, Pa. Do you want to come and have some supper?" He tried to contain his feelings as he turned to go downhill. Was there any place he could stop and think about what Francie's new life would mean to him? He had Lottie, such as she was, and the babies, but that would be all. No more kids for them as long as he would have anything to say. And, if he were very lucky, maybe Lottie would get tired of him and go back to North Carolina.

"What's gotten into him?" Rich emptied the cooling tub, half watching Lou's back as he left.

"Ah, him and that shrew wife of his are always arguing these days. I wish I could ship her somewhere." Sonny rinsed out a jar and poured some of the liquid into it. "He'll be okay, tomorrow."

It was a good summer. Francie loved her new life, her in-laws, and her wonderful, gentle, hard-working husband. By Fall, they were expecting a baby and their joy was immeasurable.

In November, Mr. and Mrs. Clark, who were almost in their fifties, drove out to California to visit their daughter, Kaye, realized they appreciated the always warm climate, and decided to stay there. Mr. Clark hadn't always been a farmer. He had made a career change in nineteen twenty-six when a long-lost uncle passed away and left him the house and fifty acres near the top of Stonesthrow Mountain.

Several ridges led to the very top. The property provided all of their needs. There were logs for building and cash, a garden large enough for a yearlong's supply of vegetables, a peach, apple and pear tree, and he kept an old mule for logging and planting, and tending the tobacco allotment. The creek wound lazily around three sides of the land that the house and the barn sat on.

One winter morning, the wood stove in the parlor, which had been banked all night, warmed the whole house right away, making the kitchen toasty. Francie was in a flannel nightgown, cooking breakfast sausage. The aroma made Hodges' mouth water as he came in the back door, arms full of firewood.

Francie looked at him and laughed.

"What's the matter?" He put the wood in the metal basket near the stove.

"You look so funny. Your nose is red from the cold."

He took off his gloves and jacket and hung them on the hook by the door. He came up behind her and put his arms around her.

"I'll remember this moment forever." He kissed her hair,

her neck and the side of her face. He went to the table and sat down as she put his eggs and sausage in front of him. He could have gotten very romantic at that moment but Brinksy was coming over to borrow some baling wire and Hodges knew he would be there very soon. He and Francie chatted about choosing baby names as they ate, and his heart was filled with love and joy.

To Francie, the mountains were always beautiful no matter the season, but in the Spring they outdid themselves with wildflowers of every kind.

"Put him up there," she cried. "At the top. That way, he'll be closer to Heaven."

He hadn't the heart to refuse her even when she insisted on climbing the ridge with him.

"But Francie," he asked, "are you sure you're strong enough?" His face was lined with concern. It had only been three days since she gave birth to the boy they named Emory, and although he'd made a valiant effort his tiny body wasn't strong enough to sustain life. He had passed away this morning just before dawn.

Hodges had hoped the baby would make it but on the second day he knew it was a losing battle. While Mrs. Kroeger, the midwife from Newport, tended to Francie and the baby, he spent a few hours in the barn fashioning a tiny casket.

When it was over, Francie washed and dressed the baby, wrapped him in the patchwork quilt she'd made for him during the winter, and put him gently into the box. Too numb for tears she felt she put her heart and soul in there with him. When Hodges closed the box they stood there, hand in hand, heads bowed, each in his own thoughts.

His stooped shoulders belied his height. His sand-colored hair looked black in the shadowed bedroom and his usually bright brown eyes were a coal black. His work boots sounded heavy on the wooden floor as he lifted the tiny casket and carried it to the porch.

His wife, still weak from childbirth, slipped on a faded blue dress and flat shoes. Her long auburn hair was still tousled from being up most of the night, and her lack of interest in combing it was poignant to Hodges.

They climbed the ridge slowly. He strained under the weight of the box and the shovel, still trying to guide her by holding onto her hand. It was steep going. Near the top she used the shovel as a crutch. He had remembered to bring a short coil of rope and he tied it around the casket and pulled and tugged it up to the flat, flower-filled summit of the ridge.

The Spring sun was strong and warm up there. Francie leaned against a hickory sapling a few feet from the top while he finished getting the baby up. When he was satisfied as to the best location he went back and helped her the rest of the way. He started to dig as she walked to the edge of the ridge, looked up to Heaven, and the tears finally began.

He was sweating from the exertion but he knew, instinctively, not to interrupt her release. He dug harder, thinking with each pitch of the shovel how much he loved this broken-hearted woman who had gone through so much in such a short time. He knew he would do everything he could to make her smile again.

While Francie stood crying in the warm sunlight, Hodges tenderly lowered the tiny box into the ground and began covering it with the moist mountain soil. Every so often he looked over at her. Her young body was wracked by sobs, her head shaking back and forth as if the events of the past few days, and now, this, could not be happening. When he finished, he walked over to her, wrapped his arms around her, buried his head in her neck and cried with her.

After awhile he said, "I can make a cross, Francie. I'll bring it up tomorrow."

She looked at him as though she were seeing him for the first time. She wiped her hand across his cheek. "Poor Hodges. Your first born. I'm so sorry." She began to sob.

"We'll have more," he promised. "Let's go home. The angels have him, now."

For awhile, Francie climbed the ridge almost every day to talk to her baby and pick flowers to lay on his tiny grave, to try to shed some of the grief that was almost too hard to bear.

At night, he would hold her as though he were drowning, gathering strength from her to go on. They'd lie together in the mountain darkness, not speaking, consoling each other through their embrace. And it worked. One day, the chores necessary for survival took over and they were all right again. To his knowledge, she didn't climb the ridge anymore.

"Leta, come on, Honey." Martha Stevens urged her little girl to hurry. The bus was leaving for Sevierville and Leta was trying to buckle her Maryjanes, which had come open. She fastened her shoe, primped her pretty party dress, and ran over to her mother.

The ride up to the Smokies was long and tiring over the twisting, turning, narrow roads, but Leta had her little face almost glued to the window. She was thrilled at the prospect of the first bus trip in her young life and could hardly tear her eyes away as the ride took them up and up into the mountains that had been only a backdrop in the distance.

"Sit down, Leta." Her mother admonished her. "Be careful not to wrinkle your dress too much."

"Yes, Ma'am. Mama, where are we going?" Leta wasn't used to getting dressed up so prettily. She loved her new blue dress and patent leather shoes. She even had a tiny patent leather purse, which held her handkerchief and five cents her mother had given her for being such a good girl when they had gone shopping last week. She played with the strap on the purse as she spoke.

"We're going to visit your Great-aunt Ruth, your Daddy's last surviving relative. If things work out, maybe you can stay and visit with her awhile." Martha was worried. John hadn't had any life insurance when he was killed in a car crash and Martha was finding it harder and harder to make ends meet. She had staked her last twenty-five dollars on Leta's pretty little outfit and this bus ride, hoping that if her cute little daughter impressed Aunt Ruth enough she would let her live with her for awhile until Martha could get a job and save enough to make another home for them.

It was a short walk from the bus terminal to Aunt Ruth's. She lived in a little cottage painted a crisp white, with blue shutters, and flower boxes filled with pansies on each windowsill. The lawn was lush and green, neatly mowed, with flowering bushes here and there, bordering the paved walkway to the front door.

Aunt Ruth met them at the door and ushered them to seats on the wicker furniture on the porch. A short, plump lady with snow-white hair and silver-rimmed eyeglasses, in a silky dress of mint green, with tiny white flowers in the print, she smelled like lavender when Martha kissed her hello. She had a tray of lemonade and sugar cookies waiting there, which she served right away.

Leta was busy choosing cookies while Martha and Aunt Ruth talked. They veiled several things in their conversation so Leta wouldn't know she was the topic.

"The problem," Aunt Ruth was saying, "is that I have such a kink in my back I go to therapy three times a week. There'd be no one here."

Martha knew that Aunt Ruth had had an accident years before, so this was plausible.

She also knew Aunt Ruth had been rumored not to like children very much.

"Please, Aunt," Martha tried very hard to present her case. "There is a man who has been trying to get me to marry him and I'm not sure if that's the right thing for me and Leta, and I'd like to wait awhile before I decide. Leta is a good little girl.

She wouldn't be any trouble. She could even help you around the house. For your back, I mean."

They discussed the pros and cons all afternoon and when it was nearly five, Aunt Ruth invited them into the house to have some supper.

Leta saw that it was neat and clean, with sheer white curtains on the windows, and pretty pictures on the walls. The dark furniture shone and was reflected in the shiny waxed linoleum as they went into the kitchen. Aunt Ruth made them chicken and dumplings, greens and cornbread, and when they had eaten she let Leta help dry the dishes, which were lovely, with blue and white birds painted on them. Leta hoped someday to have a house like that, with lovely dishes, too.

Martha was subdued on the ride back to Knoxville, and Leta slept almost all of the way. They never saw Aunt Ruth again. After awhile, Leta wasn't sure that it hadn't been a dream. Whether it was or not, Leta hung on to that dream through the years, the memory of it growing more and more perfect in her thoughts as time went by.

It wasn't long after the trip to the mountains that Martha married Robert Hollis, more out of necessity, than interest. He was the superintendent of a six-family apartment house and Martha and Leta moved into his shabby basement apartment, which he received for a reduced rent. During the day, he worked at a lumber mill and begrudged both jobs.

In time, he and Martha welcomed a little boy they named Bobby. Bobby required a lot of attention, and it soon became evident that he had some sort of mental challenge. He sucked his thumb long after the age for that had passed, and he stood on the front porch of the building, rocking back and forth on his feet for hours at a time. This only added to the frustration in the marriage.

It became a habit of Robert's to get drunk on payday, and blame his lot in life on Martha, who took to drinking, too. Often, when he was drunk he would slap Martha around and as tiny and puny as she was compared to him, she would fight back.

There was so much dissension, Leta was afraid to have any friends or socialize with anyone in case they would discover what her home life was like. Because he was a male and named after his father, her stepbrother annoyed Leta just by being there and she wanted nothing to do with him. She grew up lonely and isolated in the middle of the city.

As a witness to the constant turmoil between husband and wife she determined to better her lot in life. Her one consolation was her memory of the trip to Aunt Ruth's. That had been a far cry from the odor of stale beer and cigarettes, which permeated their Knoxville apartment now.

When Leta was sixteen her mother's brother, Uncle Toby, bought a small cafe near her home and asked her to work for him. Failing tenth grade, anyway, she quit school and became the sole employee of "Toby's Fine Food Cafe." She worked long hours for little pay and hoped to save enough for a bus to anywhere.

Although she only slept at home, Hollis demanded rent from Leta, which left her with very little money. Her family life, always tenuous, almost ceased to exist. She had no contact with any of them, including her mother, who was usually drunk, and Leta constantly thought of the day she would be able to leave.

The best part of any day at Toby's was right after the lunch crowd had left. Leta would go out onto the back porch to hang a damp towel over the railing, and stand there awhile, drinking in the splendor of the majestic peaks of the great Smokies, tall and green in the distance, and long for the peace and comfort they promised.

Georgie's father had deeded him three acres across the creek at the back of their farm. Georgie spent his high school summers building a small cabin for he and Ada to live in when they were married. On Sundays, after church, Ada would spend the day there with him, sewing curtains and slipcovers, using her mother's old treadle sewing machine, humming as she worked.

Georgie never tired of Ada's good humor and willing ways to turn the tiny house into a home. He promised himself that he'd do whatever it took to one day build Ada a fine brick ranch house.

The wedding, the day after graduation, was the highlight of the neighbors' busy days. It was the first time Francie had been out after losing the baby and she was glad to see her old friends again. Some people from school came, and her brother, Billy, and his country band supplied the music for the reception. The celebration at the Parish House lasted until the moon was high in the sky. Georgie quipped to Reverend Johnson that he'd need a bigger pick-up to cart all of the gifts home. He made arrangements to leave some of the larger items there until he could pick them up. He didn't need any of them. He had his Ada. His dream had finally come true.

After they left the party, it seemed that they dropped off the face of the earth. Mrs. Wightman had rented a chalet in Gatlinburg for them for a week. When they came home they delighted in each other's company, setting up their new place and planning for the future.

A few months later, Francie discovered she was pregnant again. She had some apprehension until she learned that Ada would be due just a month later than she. They designed layettes and discussed baby names. They agreed to exchange babysitting chores when the time came. They were so happy they made everyone around them happy.

But Francie's happiness was short-lived. Her second little boy was born three weeks early and just not strong enough to make it. She and Hodges named him Henry after her Grandfather. Hodges built another tiny box. She wrapped him in a quilt she'd made for him, kissed him goodbye, and

watched from the porch as Hodges took him to sleep forever
next to his older brother, since, this time, Francie wasn't
strong enough to climb the ridge.

As much of a blow that losing him was, Francie and
Hodges were both dismayed to have the doctor warn them
not to have any more children as Francie's life would be in
danger.

Ada and Georgie had two more in the next three years.
Their two boys and a girl soon made the cabin crowded and
Georgie decided to get a good-paying job at a slipper factory
in Knoxville, to try to save for that brick ranch house he
wanted to give Ada.

Ada drove him down the mountain to the bus every
Monday morning and picked him up on Friday evenings.
Little did she know he often hitchhiked to try to save even a
little more. Or that the boarding house he stayed in was
nothing more than a fleabag hotel in the worst part of town.
She tried to convince him that she was happy just the way
things were but his mind was made up. He figured that, in one
more year, he'd have enough saved, and he'd be home for
good.

One rainy, wintry Friday, Georgie picked up his pay,
packed his laundry in his duffle bag and headed home. The
cold rain chilled him to the bone. He pulled his cap down over
his ears, tugged his collar up, and trudged along the dark
highway, head down, and one hand holding a hopeful thumb
up.

That moonless night, a tractor-trailer, hauling produce, hit
a slick spot on the road, slid across the four lanes and slammed
into a van going the other way. The van, spun around by the
impact, came to a stop, horn blaring, with two wheels hanging
over the bridge on the north side of the Little Pigeon River. No
one had even seen Georgie, who'd been caught between the
two vehicles.

Ada had no real time to grieve, left alone with three babies. She bought a Jersey cow at an auction that Bubba Baker took her to, some laying hens from Ruby Carroll, in town, and traded milk, butter and eggs for things she needed, or repairs to the cabin. The neighbors on Stonesthrow took up a collection and bought her a sewing machine. Her only problem was finding the time to sew, trying to tend the three youngsters and the farm.

About a month after Georgie's death, his mother, Mrs. Crewe, came to call. A tiny woman, with her gray hair in a bun pinned at the nape of her neck, whose arms were as thin as parchment paper, but whose resolve and determination were as strong as any mountaineer's, came to visit her grandchildren. Ada was delighted to see her again. They sat at the kitchen table and Ada made some tea.

"I was talking to Carol and her husband, Jim, whom we all call "Bud." They decided to come back and live on the farm."

That'll be nice." Ada always thought the best, first.

"No, I don't think so." Her mother-in-law twisted the napkin in her hands. "I never really got along with Carol, and I guess Bud's okay, but they have all of these big plans about remodeling the house. Now, you know Georgie's dad had that house built for me, and I don't think I could stand to live in it if it's all changed around."

"Oh, Dear." Ada reached over and patted the woman's hands. She could see the tears starting to form in her eyes.

"I was wondering if I could come and live with you and the babies. I would help you raise your kids so you could sew, seeing you have such a gift for it."

Tears of gratitude filled Ada's eyes. "I've been praying for an answer. It is so hard to take care of the kids and the animals and do everything. I promise you that if you do come and live here, I will guarantee you a home for the rest of your life, Mother."

She got up and hugged the older woman. By now, they were both crying tears of joy. It was the beginning of a beautiful partnership. Mrs. Crewe, with her Irish looks and ways, reminded Ada so much of Georgie, it was as though his spirit was in the home with her, making her less lonely.

For Mrs. Crewe it was a chance to be needed again, to feel the satisfaction that comes with knowing you're helping someone. She delighted in her three lively grandchildren, Georgie, Jr., Elaine and Tony. They loved having their Grandma near.

Charlie Keene, a now retired over-the-road truck driver, met his schoolteacher wife, Marybelle Becker at a bluegrass festival in Newport when they were in their early thirties. They'd both come from inner-city poverty, worked hard to make a better life for themselves, had each had a bad early marriage which ended shortly after it had begun, and were not eager to repeat the mistake.

Charlie, an easy-going, gentle man, who hated confrontation, became a talented talker who could usually get someone to side with him in a debate. He debated Marybelle into agreeing they should correspond, then date, then marry. Marybelle, a short, pudgy woman with an infectious laugh was finally convinced, and they tied the knot at a little church in Kentucky.

Shortly after their wedding, on one of his cross-country trips, Charlie met an employee of the EP Lumber Company, which had, among its many holdings, a huge property on Stonesthrow Ridge. He told Charlie that the company was selling off some acreage near the top of the road. When Charlie told Marybelle, it didn't take them long to decide that moving up on the mountain would give them a whole new way of life.

Charlie bought eight acres, two of which were in a horseshoe shape that bordered the end of the road, touching the Cutter farm on the opposite side. He had a two-bedroom house built where they lived from March until November.

During the cold, snowy winters they stayed with Marybelle's sister, Rose, who lived in the valley, so Marybelle would be able to get to school to teach when the roads were bad. When they both retired they finally began living on Stonesthrow full time.

The mountains afforded them a peaceful, happy existence, and they were a welcome addition to the small community. Marybelle had a few students she tutored at home, while Charlie spent his days puttering, keeping the place up, trying his hand at whittling, and visiting with the neighbors at Bubba's.

Charlie wouldn't say he was superstitious but he couldn't help but wonder if the intense, terrible weather they had that Spring had anything to do with Georgie's accident, as though the mountain was angry at the loss. Whatever the cause, it seemed one heavy storm after another battered the area, even causing some tornado watches to be advised.

The placid branch that crossed the top of the mountains from North Carolina and passed by the Cutters' still, casually wound down his ridge to the road, merged with another small stream under the tiny wooden bridge before it cut straight across the middle of the Crewe property. It crossed the road again and usually flowed calmly and gently through the countryside, twisting and winding around the base of the Clark land on three sides before it continued on down the mountain to unite with other branches and eventually become the Little Pigeon River.

Lem Clark's old uncle had studied the course of the stream many years before and decided to build his mule's lean-to shed on the very edge of the creek so the animal could get his own drinking water. It was a low building but it had a loft where hay used to be kept. The house was further up the ridge, with a large barn directly behind it. Hodges had to park his car across the creek since all they had was a tiny footbridge.

Francie and Hodges spent many a summer evening sitting on their front porch, watching fireflies and listening to the soft, gurgling sounds of the tiny creek, as it trickled by.

One particular night, after it had rained for several days, twigs, branches and debris dammed up one of the small streams above them and turned the creek into a raging torrent. The waterway gushed and tumbled angrily down the mountain rising six feet as it roared along, cutting a wide swath through their paddock, pushing everything in its path in front of it. The flood receded rapidly but its effects were visible everywhere.

Hodges awoke to discover that their sow, a mule, two hens and their border collie were stranded in the old hayloft. He was especially disappointed to find that the swollen creek had pushed his car into the creek bed, flipping it over and carrying it downstream. It had become wedged against the mountainside when the water took a sharp turn toward the valley below.

It took awhile for the tow truck to arrive from Sevierville. The road by their place was so narrow all the man could do was park in the middle of it, unwind his cable to the end and hook it to the car. He wound and wound and pulled and tugged. For a while, it seemed as though the car would never come loose. Finally, with a mighty shake of the winch it was rescued from the water.

Hodges convinced the man to help get the distressed animals down from the loft.

Charlie was on his way home from Baker's store and finding the road blocked, opened a soft drink, put down his tailgate, and sat there to watch the operation.

It was a sight to Charlie.

The truck was parked up on the road with the driver winding and winding and pretty soon, a sow, and the next thing, a mule, and then, a dog seeming to fly through the air. He was impressed as to how gently they were deposited on the grass. All the while, the mule's braying, the sow's squealing and the dog's barking. By the time it was finished they were all laughing so hard they had tears in their eyes.

When the job was over, the man drove up to the Crewe's driveway and made a u-turn. As he passed by on his way back to town, he waved to Hodges, Francie and Charlie, still laughing.

From that day on, Charlie would tell anyone who'd listen about the time the mountain cried over Georgie.

"I'll be away today." Sonny's words always sounded defiant, as though he dared anyone to argue with him.

Lottie stared into space as she drank her coffee. In her mind, she was saying, "Good! That's one less day I have to put up with you, Old Man."

Lou said, "Where you going, Pa?"

"Buster Roberts wants me to deliver a load of logs for him."

"Where to?" Lou and Sonny acted as though Lottie wasn't there.

She got up took her coffee, and slammed the door as she went out on the porch. It had been quite awhile since the three of them had been civil to each other. She really didn't care where either of them went.

"It's over to Hidden Hollow, to that KB Paper Company."

"Well, I heard of it, but it's way back in the mountains, isn't it?" Lou was not sure.

Sonny answered, "Yeah! About thirty miles from here, on the other side of Cherokee Ridge. It's a good day's pay, and it'll keep these nosy neighbors off our trail." He finished tying his work boots and stood up and tucked his shirt in his pants. He gave Lou as near to a smile as he was capable of, although, to Lou, it looked more like a smirk.

"Then I'll go up and make sure Jimmie Blake dumped the rest of the mash in." Lou looked toward the porch. "She's getting harder and harder to live with, Pa."

The mountain man's steely look told Lou that he didn't want to hear it. He hated Lottie for trapping Lou into marriage, neither one took much care of the children, and if it wasn't for he, Sonny, the three boys would be totally wild. As it was now, Sonny was their main disciplinarian, and he ruled them as he had Lou, through fear and intimidation. He put on his cap and left.

Lou left shortly after without a word to Lottie, who was in her usual place these days, sitting on the old cane rocker on the porch, staring at the mountains in the distance. It reminded Lou so much of his poor dead mama sitting there he almost shuddered as he went by. At least, Lottie was drinking coffee and she could speak, although she wouldn't if she didn't absolutely have to.

When he left, Lottie went back in the house and turned on her favorite soap opera. The sound came in but the picture was almost impossible to watch.

"These blasted mountains!" She couldn't wait to get away from this place, the Cutter men, and even her three annoying sons, who had stolen her youth and her looks. "One of these days," she pacified herself. She almost had enough money to leave. She started packing a small suitcase, which she kept hidden under the bed.

Buster was one of the few men Sonny liked. He used to buy pelts from Sonny when Sonny was a trapper living on Cherokee Ridge. They went back a long time, together, always dealing squarely with each other.

Over the years, Buster decided to log his own timber, using a mule, and once in awhile, he'd hire some of the young boys who lived on the mountains to help him get the logs down from the tall ridges. It cost him money and time to deliver the logs to a sawmill, himself, so when he had a truckload he would call Sonny. Sonny felt it made him seem legitimate to the other residents on Stonesthrow, so they wouldn't discover that his real business was moonshining.

It took Sonny quite awhile to drive the heavy truckload around the mountain roads, until he finally climbed the steep hill to the factory. He looked for the delivery gate but there were three entrances. Unsure of which one to drive through, he put the emergency brake on and climbed down from the cab. At six foot four, he was an imposing figure as he strode past the side of the truck towards the rear.

The shifting of the load from driving around the hairpin turns had worn the braces through and some of them snapped, causing several of the logs to fall at that exact moment, burying Sonny. The rumbling racket was deafening.

The guard at the gate saw the whole thing and radioed for help as he ran to the truck. The ambulance men thought Sonny was dead until he moaned.

"I'm going to get some 'taters," Francie called, as she opened the front door.

Her soft warm voice enveloped him. The words she spoke always seemed to Hodges to be wrapped in a smile, a gentle, calming smile. They had grown up together and he knew from the beginning that he wanted the sound of her voice in his life. He pulled up the straps on his overalls as he reached the front door. Francie was down the three porch steps and almost to the garden by the time he stepped outside.

The early morning was damp with humidity. It would be a hot day. The mountains were above him, tall, and timbered, as his eyes swept the horizon. They were a part of his soul. He knew no other place nor did he want to. His beloved mountains. His beloved Francie. He stood there awhile drinking in the scene, and said a little prayer of thanksgiving just as Francie called his name.

The dew was heavy on the grass and she knew the potatoes would come out easily.

74

It made her think of a prospector digging for gold. Her fingers sifted through the dark moist ground, finding one "golden nugget" after another. She was on her knees, stretching across the lush foliage of the plants, plucking, then passing each potato to the wooden basket she had brought with her. She enjoyed the day's promise of heat on her face as she thought about how many potatoes to gather for the annual neighborhood picnic the following day.

Years ago, there was a big crowd, but since most of the youngsters had gone off on their own, the attendance was down to a small group of older families who still lived on Stonesthrow. It would be good to be with them again. Springtime had been particularly hectic this year, and except for church no one had much time for visiting. They all looked forward to the yearly event between planting season and tobacco tending, and each contributed to its success.

She leaned a little further over the plants and saw the snake before she felt the sting.

Copperhead!

She drew her hand back instinctively, and jumped up. Hodges! She thought she imagined his name. She actually screamed it in a voice he'd never heard before.

Hodges ran to the garden just as she reached the fencerow and collapsed in a heap at his feet. He picked her up and saw her left hand bleeding in two tiny places. He knew right away what had happened and carried her across the creek, put her into the truck, jumped in, and began driving as fast as the winding mountain road would let him.

Bubba Baker took his daily walk out to the mailbox to retrieve the newspapers, which had just been delivered to his store. He breathed in the fresh mountain air, smiling at the panoramic scene below where the mountain met the valley.

Farms spread out in perfect symmetry as far as he could see, with the tall mountains encircling the scene, green patches of crops, golden fields of hay, cornfields, neat clapboard homes, now and then a brick ranch house, large barns, livestock grazing, keeping their balance on the sides of the steep ridges, deep dark woods rising opposite the winding two-lane road which curled and twisted down from the summit, until it met the county road which ran a straighter course along the creek, where both widened when they reached the main highway. It was a view he relished every morning.

He picked up the bundle and was just about to return to the store when a dark blue pick-up truck sped past the intersection, coming from the top of the road and barely pausing at the stop-sign before revving the engine and taking off down the winding road towards the valley. He looked on in amazement. That was Hodges Clark's truck and he was always such a careful driver. Something must have happened.

As the truck made its way down the winding two-lane road, Francie was at the mercy of the curves and was bounced from side to side. Hodges, white-faced and resolute, tried to steady his wife with his free arm as much as he could. On some of the tighter turns, he had to hold on to the wheel with both hands to keep the truck on the road, and she would bob again, moaning in pain. Francie was slipping in and out of consciousness as they drove. There was a slight clacking noise in the engine, and in her foggy brain she remembered that sound.

It was the last day of school before Spring break. Francie was in the sixth grade. The Tennessee sun hadn't come overhead yet, making the day gray from the cloud that had settled over the mountain top, but the humidity was high enough to get a little done in the vegetable garden.

Most of the land was in timber so they had no choice but to till this few acres. The potatoes had been planted a few weeks before and it was time to start the peas and green beans. They had to work early before the sun came up and baked the soil.

Her two older brothers were flipping rocks over the ridge they lived on to the creek far below and listening for the clacking sound they made as they struck the rocks already down there. She couldn't throw that far so they wouldn't let her join in. She just threw hers into a small pile she'd been making in a corner of the field.

Once, she had asked her Mama if there were such a thing as Rock Fairies, who came in the night and put them back there, because it seemed that no matter how many rocks they threw away, the next day there were so many more.

Her Mother used the hoe to smooth out the furrows that her Father was plowing with their old white mule, Loopy. Her Father had a rhythm going with Loopy, up one row and down the next, turning sharply before the line of trees that overlooked the road below their land.

"Gee! Gee!" her Father unexpectedly yelled to the mule, but he had come to a dead stop and stood there, obstinately refusing to move. The plow had caught the edge of a very large rock buried under the soil and the blade was stuck, unable to move either forward or back.

They all ran over to help. Mr. Mann kept jockeying the plow, talking to the mule to either "gee," or "haw". It took several minutes before there was any progress and they were all straining with the heat of the work.

All of a sudden, the boulder came loose, the blade of the plow snapped free, and their father went flying headlong into the dirt, while the mule, feeling the slack now, began once more to walk the furrow.

"Whoa! You mangy critter!" Her Father yelled as he stood up. His overalls were covered with black dirt. It was in his hair and on his eyeglasses. He removed them and reached in his back pocket for his handkerchief, wiping them off. He looked so funny, the kids began to laugh and soon, they were all laughing.

"You get on," he pretended to scold. "It's time for school."

The sun was high, now. They washed up and headed down the road to school, which was just about a mile from Baker's grocery store on the county highway.

That was a long time ago.

As Hodges sped along the scent of wildflowers wafted through Francie's blunted senses. She recalled how the Mountain Laurels were heavy with blooms that year. The Queen Anne Lace grew in such profusion, as if trying to crowd out the Daisies and Black-eyed Susans that bordered the road.

In her dulled mind she still heard that clacking sound. She drifted off again.

"I can't wait to tell Ada what happened," Francie smiled through her pain.

She could see Ralph shuffling his feet in the sand alongside the road. "I hate that stupid stone throwing! When I get older, I'm gonna live in a big city, maybe even New York, and get away from these big ol' mountains."

Billy thought out loud. "When I get older, I want to go to Nashville and be a big country music star."

Francie ignored Ralph. His complaining was almost a habit. "I'll bet you will be, Billy." her voice was so low he struggled to hear her.

"What, Francie?"

"Everybody around here liked the way you sang at the church social. And you play the guitar so well." She was closer to Billy and he often played the peacemaker between Francie and Ralph, who felt, by way of being the oldest, that he had the right to boss her around.

"I guess." Billy was modest but he enjoyed the compliment.

Ralph was jealous. "Shut up, you two, here come the rest of the kids."

There were the two Crewe children, Georgie and Carol, Lou Cutter, and the twin Clark girls who were seniors in high school, with their younger brother, Hodges, who was in Ralph's class. The older students waited on the corner for the bus, which would take them down to the high school in the valley.

Ada Wightman, who was Francie's best friend, lived on the other side of the county highway. She always met her at Bubba's and walked with her.

Georgie and Ada had met the very first day of Kindergarten. He took one look at her and fell hopelessly in love. Everyone teased Ada, calling her "Idy", except Georgie, who said "Ada Sue" with almost a reverence in his tone.

She took right to Georgie, too. A soft-spoken girl with long straight blonde hair, Ada paid close attention to her clothes and the bright colored dresses she wore seemed to fill her with a certain cheerfulness.

Her Mama made all of her dresses and was teaching Ada to sew.

Everyone respected her mother, Mrs. Wightman, a widow, who sheared sheep belonging to her neighbors, dyed the wool with the colors she boiled out of wildflowers, spun the yarn and then, wove it into fine rugs and tapestries, selling her wares at the tourist stores in Gatlinburg. Ada loved to go up on the high ridges with her to gather blueberries and raspberries and wildflowers.

Georgie, a good-natured boy who favored his Irish mother, with red hair, a freckled-face, and a contagious smile, could often be seen walking the few miles from his house to Ada's, especially on the weekends.

Ada informed anyone who'd listen that when she and Georgie grew up they would be married.

Francie said, "I wonder who I'll ever marry?"

Charlie squinted as he entered Bubba's. "That sun sure is bright today." He removed his cap and hung it on a hook near the door.

Bubba was untying and sorting the newspapers. "What do you expect when you come in in the middle of the day?" They had been teasing each other for a long time.

"You think I'm late? Here comes Brinksy." Charlie poured himself a cup of coffee. "I'm having one," Charlie explained, as he walked over to the corner, "to celebrate." He sat on one of the folding chairs that were lined up against the wall.

"What are we celebrating?" Bubba stopped what he was doing and came over to the man.

"Dang! Ain't anybody here anymore to celebrate with." Charlie sipped the hot liquid.

"Are you saying you sold your land?" Brinksy was immediately enthusiastic, as he rushed to the counter and began rifling through the new papers. "Wait'll I check this. Nah! It ain't here. Maybe tomorrow."

"Yeah! The Mann family moved away. So did Lem Clark. Ol' man Cutter ain't been here in a long time, so it's just us, unless Hodges comes in. You sold your farm?" Bubba cut in.

"Pa Cutter wouldn't want to hear what I have to say. It's good he don't come anymore. I sold those two acres down by the road that border his place. And I'm glad. He always makes me think of fence posts, tall and long-standing, but rotten at the core.

"And I'm also glad that Lou wasn't home when the man came to look at it. Anyways, he liked it and he bought it, but he won't come and build on it for a few years until he retires, so that'll give Lou a chance to get used to the idea. Those Cutters are bad eggs and I want to have that buffer between us. You know Lou and his Pa think land is the only thing that matters.

"You heard that story, didn't ya? About his ancestors?"

"I did, but I don't think Brinksy did, did you?" Bubba looked at his old friend.

"Yeah! Lou's pa and that floozy wife of Lou's had Evelyn's ear when we had the picnic at our place." Brinksy removed his bifocals and put them in his pocket "Speaking of Pa Cutter, leave it to him to get into trouble."

"Don't tell me his still got raided?" Bubba perked up at this. They all suspected Sonny had a still somewhere on the ridges but no one ever confronted him about it because they weren't really sure. But Bubba knew. He had sometimes ordered large quantities of sugar for Sonny. In return, he often received a jar of what he called "medicine."

"The postman just stopped and told me. His neighbor is an emergency ambulance man and he got a call yesterday to go to Hidden Hollow. That's about thirty miles south of Cherokee Ridge where Sonny come from. It seems he had a job for that paper outfit over there, I think it's called the KB Company. Anyways, he stopped to check the road sign thinking he had passed his turn by and when he walked past the side of the truck a brace snapped and several of the logs fell on him.

"The postman's neighbor told him Sonny's in a bad way and if he lives he'll be severely crippled." Brinksy shook his head in sympathy.

"Well, he's been a crotchety old goat ever since I met him and now that he's been hurt, he's probably even worse. I have no doubt he'll make it, he's too ornery not to. I'm glad that land is sold. As I said, I'll be glad to have a buffer between us." Charlie put his cup down. "He won't be making anymore booze for awhile. Gotta get home. Marybelle needs to hear all the news. See ya."

"Wonder where ol' Hodge is? He promised to bring me some baling twine. I have some hay to mow and bale for Widow Marsh over to Cosby and I ran out. I'd hate to have to make a trip all the way to Newport." Brinksy was curious.

"Don't know what's going on with him. When I went out to get the papers he come down the road like a madman. Didn't even stop at the stop sign. Lucky nothing was coming. You know you can check his barn if he ain't home."

"That sure don't sound like ol' Hodge. Which way was he going?" Brinksy was becoming concerned.

"Couldn't tell. He went by here so fast, I think, toward Sevierville." Bubba started making another pot of coffee. "Let me know if you hear anything."

"You, too." Brinksy left.

As the coffee brewed, Bubba wondered about his neighbors. He remembered when Sonny, his wife and young son moved over to Stonesthrow. Must have been in the mid-thirties right after Bubba and Mary opened the store. He scratched his baldhead. Don't recall ever meeting Mrs. Cutter. Word went around that she wasn't right in the head, but Bubba didn't know that for a fact.

He remembered she died when Lou was about nine or ten. He used to see young Lou when he walked to school with the other kids. They all passed right by his store every morning. None of them ever seemed friendly to him.

When the boys on Stonesthrow got big enough, Bubba and some of the other farmers in the area would hire them to help with their chores. He didn't recall anyone asking Lou to work. Must have been 'cause Sonny made it very clear that he didn't want anyone coming on his place.

And then, Lou had a wife. Must have been around the same time that Francie and Hodges eloped. Nah! It had to be a year or two earlier. He was just a kid, seventeen or so. And her! She was a looker. Really built curvy, and older than him, but what an attitude! Tried to dress like a movie star, which didn't fit these hills. That reminds me of how she started coming to the annual picnics with her three boys, but after a few times, she quit. None of the other wives liked her and they still don't.

And look where those boys are now. Bubba shook his head. None of us really know those boys, except for seeing them when they were on their way to school. And now, that Billy is in the reformatory. Just goes to show you-the apple doesn't fall far from the tree. He always seemed to be a little sneak. Truth be told, I feel better that he's locked up

When the store was empty, Bubba sat by the now quiet potbelly stove, picked up a piece of wood he had begun to whittle on and started to work on it again. He felt he did some of his best thinking as he whittled.

He remembered when he and his bride, Mary, came to Stonesthrow from eastern North Carolina, just outside of Wilmington. Mary was an asthmatic and the doctors recommended mountain air for her condition. They bought the general store, which had been in business for several years, and three acres on the opposite side of the road. They lived in the back of the store until a house was built for them over there.

Bubba had always wanted a small business, with the operative word being "small". Not particularly ambitious, he wanted something where he could do the minimal amount of work with the maximum amount of money. They decided to try the store for five years and if it didn't work out they'd go on to something else.

They'd only been open a short time when Sonny Cutter came in from Cherokee Ridge looking for directions to the old Browne place for sale up the road. Not very sociably, Sonny told Bubba and the others who were in the store that day that he was being evicted by the government, that his wife wasn't well, and his baby son was afraid of strangers, so he hoped they would all respect his wishes and leave them alone. His attitude made them more than happy to agree.

Lem Clark explained that the property in question adjoined his and he would show Sonny where it was since he was going home, anyway. When they left, Brinksy, Kent Crewe, Charlie Keene and Bubba each commented on Sonny's lack of neighborliness.

"It's going to be interesting with him up here." Tom Brinks never minced words.

"Maybe he's just having a bad time," said Bubba. "After all, having to move is not like doing it on your own thought."

"Yeah! Maybe when they get settled and get this behind them, he'll change." Brinksy was willing to give Sonny the benefit of the doubt.

But, thought Bubba, he never did change. Just got more and more ornery. And Lou's the same. And so are Lou's kids.

As he whittled, Bubba remembered Mary. She was a petite blonde, with green eyes.

He'd met her at a soda shop where she was working as a waitress. They dated a few times and decided to marry shortly after, and Bubba began shopping for a business to buy. The least expensive one he'd found was on a mountain in the Smokies, which fit right in with his plan to help Mary improve her health.

Dear little Mary, he thought, she was a gamey little thing. Always ready to go along with any of my crazy schemes. I sure do miss her.

Her asthma seemed to improve except for Spring when everything began to bloom. Sometimes, she had a really rough time of it, but she usually stayed in the house and rested, took her medicines and toughed it out. One year, nothing seemed to help, and after a strong attack, tiny little Mary passed away, begging Bubba to keep the store, knowing how much he enjoyed the business.

He couldn't stay in the house, though. Their house held too many memories for him. So he sold the place to a war widow, a Mrs. Wightman, with a little girl named Ada, and moved back in behind the store.

The years seemed to fly by and here it was nineteen sixty-six. There had been a few changes on the mountain. Several of the older kids had moved away, as had the senior Clarks, and the Mann's. Kent Crewe had also passed away, the mountain air not lessening the damage to his lungs from his stints in a West Virginia coal mine when he was a young man, as he had hoped it would. And he wasn't that old, either, Bubba realized.

And Sonny's wife died that same year as Mary. That wasn't a good year for Stonesthrow, he thought. But since then, it's been pretty good up to now. Too bad about Sonny. I reckon they'll keep him in for a while. Probably have to go to a rehab place afterward. That's if he makes it. As Charlie says, "he's too ornery to die."

About an hour later, Brinksy stopped in again.

"There's no one up to Hodges' place." he was puzzled. "Guess Francie went with him. I found the twine in the barn, though, so if they stop in on their way home from wherever they are, would you tell him I got it?"

"Wait a minute. I tried to call Lou but there's no answer."

Brinksy answered, "Didn't look like anyone was to home when I passed Lou's, either. Maybe they heard about the accident and are on their way to the hospital, although I doubt if Lou's wife would go. She's a hard one, that woman. Probably wouldn't answer the door, either."

Brinksy was trying to feel a little sympathy for Sonny, although the two had had angry words years before and had never mended that fence. "I'll ask Evelyn if she's heard anything about his condition. She can get information from her office, being the nursing supervisor at the Sevierville General Hospital, even though she took off this week for our picnic. You coming tomorrow?"

"I promised Evelyn I'd close the store from one to two and drop by for lunch After all, it's just across the road. If anyone needs anything from the store, I can run right back here."

"It won't be anything like the ones we've had all these years, now that most of the kids are grown. Still, it'll make a nice break in routine and give us a chance to just visit without having to rush to tend a crop or work on tobacco. See you later." He left again.

* * *

Hodges drove the old pick-up as fast as he could around the bends in the road, casting nervous glances at his wife. She was semi-conscious, trying to keep her balance when she wasn't sleeping, as they seemed to career off one curve and slide around another.

At one point, she sat straight up and looked out of the window. Her eyes had trouble focusing. "Is that the new bridge?" She thought she spoke aloud. "Is that Georgie's bridge?" She hadn't been this far from home in a long time. She passed out again.

Hodges put one hand on her shoulder trying to steady her as she lay across the front seat.

The hospital entrance was a welcome sight. The truck slid to a screeching halt as a young orderly rushed out of the double doors. He ran over to the truck and opened the door as another man pushed a stretcher over to him. One word said it all—"Copperhead!"

Together, they lifted the unconscious Francie onto the gurney and hurried into the building.

Hodges parked the truck in the lot across the street and ran into the hospital. He collided with two doctors who were running down the hall to attend Francie, and followed them into the cubicle in the Emergency Room only to be stopped by an elderly woman in a pink smock.

"Please, Sir, have a seat in the hall." She pointed to a row of metal chairs.

"My wife," he was frantic.

"We'll take good care of her." She ushered him to a chair and left him there. He sat, staring at the floor tiles. Once, he glanced up at the clock on the wall. It was ten-thirty. They'd been up for hours.

He took a long deep breath, leaned back against the wall and closed his eyes. His mind was on Francie.

He could see her just the other day, throwing feed to the chickens. He had stood by the fence, one leg up on the first board, just watching. She didn't know he was there at first, but when the gentle breeze blew a few tendrils of her long auburn curls into her face, and she turned around to pin them back behind her ears, she saw him. He immediately saw the huge, shy grin she reserved for him and the love in her eyes, and he was smitten all over again, as it had always been with the two of them all these years. He moaned.

The same lady came over with a clipboard and a sheet for him to fill out. She was trying to make him feel better. "Where do you live, Sir?"

"Up on Stonesthrow." That's how his part of the mountain was known throughout East Tennessee.

"I've never been up there," she said. "I hear it's hard to farm up there. Because of the rocks, I mean."

Hodges was uncharacteristically sarcastic. "That's why they call it Stonesthrow.

And our life is like that. We keep throwing off the bad things that happen to us, and the next time we turn around there are many more to try to get rid of. Will life ever be smooth and easy?"

She took the clipboard and went away without answering him.

He closed his eyes again. Church was a large part of their lives and he saw her there whenever there was a service or special event going on, but certain moments always stood out in his mind.

He could see Francie when she was a child, walking to school with Ada and Georgie, her long dark hair always trying to escape the pins her mother had tried to hold it in place with, her sparkling brown eyes, with just a flash of mischief in them, and the way they reflected a kind and sweet soul.

He saw her at thirteen, one winter night when he was visiting her brothers, and she squeezed apples for juice. She was becoming quite pretty, and she brushed his hand as she put the glass in front of him. That was the first time he thought he might have a chance to plan to have her in his life sometime in the future. Little did he know it was to be a short three years later.

For a few minutes, he opened his eyes and looked at the clock again.

Hodges was almost lost in his memories when he realized there was a lot of hustling and bustling in the hallway. He stood up and grabbed the arm of an orderly who was carrying some equipment towards the emergency room.

"What's going on?"

The young man didn't stop, but spoke as he continued on his way. "She's allergic to the anti-venin serum. We can't let it reach her heart." He hurried into the room, closing the door behind him.

As Hodges returned to his chair another young man came over to him.

"Here's a cup of coffee for you, Sir. You doing okay?"

Hodges took the coffee and said, "Thanks." He sounded beaten.

"I'll check with you in a little while," the orderly promised. "I'll try to keep you updated on your wife's condition."

The moments began to drag again as Hodges sipped the coffee. When he finished he put the cup on the floor, leaned back and closed his eyes again.

He saw Francie on their wedding day. He had come by in his nineteen thirty-six Dodge sedan, which he'd bought with money he'd earned as a day laborer. He was so proud of it. The outside shone like glass but the rear floorboards were rotted out and he'd had to put a piece of plywood from door to door. Still, it ran smoothly, and he was happy to have it.

Francie had worn a dress she wore to school, not wanting to arouse suspicion. She looked adorable. They got into the car and waved goodbye.

As they drove down the mountain, Hodges asked, "Are you nervous, Francie?"

"Not when I'm with you," she had answered, and that pleased him.

That was a long time ago.

He opened his eyes again. No one had come out to speak to him and he was becoming very worried. He walked down the hall to the nurse's desk.

"Please," his voice was hoarse. "May I see my wife?"

The nurse looked up at the tired, distraught man.

"Mr. Clark, you can go into her room now. I was just getting ready to call you. The antidote worked and your wife will be okay. But the Doctor wants her to stay a few days to be on the safe side. She will probably sleep a few hours from the medicines she's had." She smiled.

"She's in Room 157,down the hall on the right." She watched, as his tall, thin frame almost flew down the hallway.

It took less than a minute for him to pull a chair up to her bedside and hold her hand. It was late evening by now and he was bone weary. He laid his head on the bed next to her waist and fell asleep.

He awoke when he heard the nurse buzzing around Francie.

"What is it?" he asked.

"It's a change of bandage," the lady answered. "The wound has been opened more to drain the poison so it bleeds profusely. We won't have to change it many more times. It looks as if it's doing much better." She finished her work and left the room again.

Hodges looked at his sleeping wife. Her arm, wrapped in the new, clean bandage, and swollen to three times its usual size, made the rest of her body look tiny and frail, and reminded him of the reason they were here, and he swore to himself he'd get that snake if it were the last thing he ever did.

He knew how much she loved the mountains. To Francie, they were beautiful, majestic and magnificent. She loved the seasons when they changed, but she especially loved the Spring. Springtime in the mountains was a sight to behold, with all sorts of wildflowers blooming in myriad colors and sizes. He was always impressed by her wonder at Nature's bounty, but he promised himself he'd take her far away from these mountains if he had to choose between the mountains and her safety.

Francie opened her eyes, thinking she had seen a huge boar cross the road in front of their truck. She saw Hodges and wanted to tell him about the pigs but she couldn't speak. There was still some pain but she was too tired to complain about it and fell back to sleep.

She was dreaming. In her dreams she heard her father say "That damn pig!" She opened her eyes but her vision was too blurry to make out the sow, which had wandered into the road. She closed them again and was back at her Daddy's farm.

"Francie, it's your turn to feed the pigs."

She picked up the slop bucket from under the kitchen sink and walked out slowly to the pigpen, which was nothing more than slats wired together to form a circle. The piglets were under three months and thought her bare feet were their supper. They came rushing to her, squealing the whole time. When she climbed into the pen they began nipping at her toes. She tried to pour the feed into the long trough as fast as she could. Billy had followed her.

"C'mon, Sis, I'll help you," he lifted the bucket over the fence for her. He had to lean his legs against the slats so the whole fence wouldn't fall as she climbed back out.

The next day, her father moved the pen up higher on the ridge so the pigs could root out some of the undergrowth. It was a major undertaking. Billy and Ralph had to shoo the pigs into a big cage while their parents raised and moved the slats.

Francie watched, with their border collie, Corky, while the boys took the pigs out of the cage, one at a time, walking them with their back feet in the air like a wheelbarrow, and lifting them over the fence into the pen.

One of the little pigs let out a terrified squeal, which startled Billy so much, that he dropped him as he hoisted him over the fence. Billy leaned on the slats to keep his balance and the whole pen collapsed, sending the piglets running and squealing into the woods. Their dad tried to head them off but they squeezed right past him. The boys were clamoring after them scaring them even more, the dog was barking and their mother was yelling, "Get them! Get them!"

The pigs were headed downhill towards the deep woods by the creek. Mr. Mann knew one of the neighbors who lived near there would see that they returned. Francie just stood there, frozen, not knowing what to do.

Her daddy was laughing as he came over to her. He scooped her up in his arms and said, "It's okay, Baby. Don't be afraid. Those six little pigs just went to market. They'll be home by nightfall." He carried her into the kitchen and set her down on a chair. Mama gave her a nice warm biscuit.

As she munched the biscuit, Francie thought, I'm glad they're gone. Now they can't bite my feet, anymore.

"My feet," she spoke aloud for the first time in a long time.

"My feet are cold," she said, in her stupor.

Hodges sat up at the sound of her voice, optimistic for the first time. He knew she was delirious, but he was sure that being able to speak was a good sign. Another nurse had left a breakfast tray and this time, he was hungry enough to sample it.

The day of the picnic dawned rainy and wet. Evelyn Brinks, a feisty, but friendly, lady with a professional nurse's confidence and the ability to adapt to any situation, decided at the last minute to have the party inside.

She and her husband, Tom, lived just about two doors down and across the road from Bubba's store. Tom had grown up there, the son of a farmer, and the grandson of a farmer, and never wanted to be anything more than a farmer, himself. He invested in some dairy cows, got a grant from a noted dairy to build a barn and sell them the milk to make cheeses with. This was so successful, he was able to buy heavy equipment to mow, plow, plant, bush-hog and even combine when the wheat was ready, and he made a very good living at it for many years.

He had met Evelyn Joseph at a hospital fundraiser, which he hadn't wanted to attend, but he always said how glad he was that he did. She was the light of his life and they had been married over forty years. She was almost due to retire from the hospital and couldn't wait until she would have time to sit and knit and visit with their three grandchildren, who lived in Knoxville.

She also loved living on the mountain, and canned and preserved most of the food they grew in the large garden she tended. Her preserves were noted in the area and she had won several prizes for them over the years.

As Evelyn set the table she couldn't help but notice with sadness that one long table would be enough. "Nothing like it used to be," she said to her husband. She smoothed out the tablecloth, wistfully. "I remember when we needed six long tables, what with all the kids. Oh, well!"

Around eleven, Marybelle and Charlie pulled into the driveway. They both had slickers on and tried not to step in the mud as they ran to the side door. Evelyn held the storm door open for them. They came into the summer kitchen, wiped their feet and hung up their slickers. Marybelle had a sweater on.

"It's cool for July." Her exuberance was always evident and she gave a little chuckle even as she apologized for being cold. "Evelyn, I can't believe it. Where is everyone?"

She had noticed the one long table set in the dining room.

"It looks like it may just be a few of us. We don't know if Hodges and Francie are coming. They don't seem to be around. Of course, since Hodges' sisters, Kaye and Annie moved away, and the twins, Alice and Loretta, married and moved down to the valley, along with Carol Crewe and her husband, I can never remember his name, none of them have been here."

"It's Budzinski. Remember, he came from New Jersey." Marybelle wasn't known locally as the "Town Crier" for nothing.

"That's right," Evelyn agreed as she led Marybelle to a chair in the living room and they both sat. "That was when Miz Crewe bought that brand new washer and it broke and they called for service and he came up here."

"Yeah! That's when she dumped poor Billy Mann. I think she broke his heart.

That's why he left the mountain." Marybelle kicked her shoes off and wiggled her toes.

"Do you mind?" she asked. Evelyn smiled. It was known far and wide that Marybelle Keene did not like to wear shoes and usually took them off whenever it was possible.

"Of course not, Dear." They had been friends for years and Evelyn always looked forward to spending time with her whether or not she wore shoes.

"How's work, Evelyn? I hear you may be retiring soon. I often wonder since Charlie and I retired how we'd ever find time to work. There always seems to be so much to do."

"I hope by the next year or two I can leave. I had thought about traveling a little but Tom just wants to take a trip to Knoxville to see the kids and the grandkids, and I can't get him to go any further. This mountain is in his blood and I do believe he would miss it the way you'd miss a loved one. I think most of the people who still live up here feel pretty much the same way.

"How's your son, Eddie? Does he still live in Nashville? And the boys? I remember when Eddie and his friend, Annie Clark, broke all of the windows in that small greenhouse you had." Evelyn laughed. "They said it was target practice."

"Him and that Annie! Nothing like her other sisters. All tomboy, and horse crazy. I remember her stealing your old plow horse and taking him for a ride up to the top of the road. She was a caution! And who'd of thought she'd grow up to be a rodeo rider and follow the circuit? Does good, too. I hear she makes a lot of money, too, Barrel Racing."

"Remember her older sister, Kaye? She's the only one of the mountain kids who went to college. A full scholarship, too! And then, when she graduated she landed that job on that big California newspaper. She's another one making good. Somehow, we all feel like these are partly our own kids and we're so proud. Know what I mean?" Evelyn offered Marybelle some hard candies.

"No, thanks. I'll wait for lunch. Getting back to that time at the greenhouse, I told Eddie it would come out of his allowance and I don't think we ever gave him an allowance again." She laughed a loud, long laugh.

"How old are the boys, now?"

"Eddie Boy is twelve and Bobby is eleven. Did I tell you they both started Little League?"

"Well, no. How're they doing?"

Marybelle laughed to punctuate her next sentence. "Eddie says every time he turns around, it seems those boys have to go to baseball practice. I told him that if those boys went to Sunday School as often as they go to baseball practice, they'd be Heaven bound."

At that, they both laughed.

"Come and help me set the table." Evelyn got up and headed for the kitchen. "We did a hog last week," she explained, "so I thought we'd have pork chops."

"Ummm! That sounds great." Marybelle called out the door to Charlie and Brinksy, who were standing in the doorway of the barn. "Come and get it."

They waved in acknowledgment and headed to the house.

"How'd you get away from me, Charlie? I thought you hung up your slicker when I did." Marybelle smiled.

"I waited til your back was turned and went out to talk to Tom. I figured you hens had some catch-up cackling to do." He put his nose in the air. "Pork chops and sweet 'taters, my favorite foods." He sat down at the table and began to fix his plate.

Marybelle was the first to talk. "I guess y'all heard that Charlie sold that land between us and Cutter's?"

"I'll bet you're happy." Tom Brinks fixed his plate.

"Yes! But I do think Charlie could have gotten more money for it. It's a nice piece of land, with all those shade trees and the creek directly by. Not like the rocky land we have over yonder."

Charlie took a huge bite out of the juicy meat. As he chewed, he said to Evelyn, "This meat sure is tender. The last pigs we did up were on the tough side. Did you make some bacon, too? And hams?"

When Evelyn nodded in agreement, he continued, "I may buy a couple from you. Although I did see down in the valley, at Pinky's grocery, they're advertising the hog jowls for thirty-nine cents a pound. It almost makes you wonder if we shouldn't just buy it ready to eat."

"Last time Charlie butchered our pigs I think the only part he didn't use was the grunt," said Marybelle. They all laughed together.

"Seriously, I think Charlie could have done better with that sale. He's just too good-natured. Always has been."

Evelyn thought she'd tease Charlie a little. "Do you hear what she's saying, Charlie? Are you gonna let her get away with that?"

"Yeah! For now." His mouth was shiny with grease. He pointed the pork chop at Marybelle, who sat opposite. He gave her a hard stare, all the while shaking that pork chop like some big Cherokee chief and said, softly and calmly, "Let her go on. When I get her down the road, I'm gonna whip her."

Everyone knew Charlie was kidding. He and Marybelle had recently celebrated their thirtieth anniversary and they were very happy together.

Brinksy surprised everyone when he said, "Did anyone hear how Sonny's doing?"

Evelyn had heard the night before.

"No," Charlie became serious right away.

"Oh, here's Bubba. We'll let him tell you."

Bubba rushed in out of the rain. "Am I too late? Boy, that sure smells good." He wiped his feet and came in and sat down. "Oh, no, I haven't heard anymore. I think Lou and his wife might have gone to the hospital. At any rate, the postman stopped at the store and said no one was home when he brought the mail up."

Evelyn spoke up. "I doubt if Lou's wife would go with him, but she wouldn't open the door, either."

"Yeah! Miss High and Mighty." Charlie spoke for all of them, but he and Marybelle were still in the dark.

Bubba went on as he fixed his plate. "Sonny had an accident with a log truck. He'll probably be laid up a long time, if he makes it."

Marybelle felt a sudden rush of sympathy. "Should I bring some food up there to Lou and his family? Is there anything we can do?"

"That's my Honey." Charlie looked from face to face to make sure they knew what he was thinking. They all agreed. Marybelle was always there in a pinch. "But I don't think you ought to bother. You know Lou's wife. She don't want anyone up there. And if Sonny heard, he'd be even more angry and bitter than he usually is." He went back to his food.

"Charlie's right, Marybelle," Evelyn agreed. "They know if they need any help all they have to do is ask. Now, how about some of that delicious pie you brought." She went into the kitchen to get it.

Just then, the phone rang.

When Evelyn returned to the dining room she seemed upset.

"What is it, Dear?" Marybelle was instantly concerned.

"That was Miss Meyers, one of my Pink Lady volunteers at the hospital. She thought I'd like to know that one of my neighbors on Stonesthrow has been admitted."

"Sonny?" Charlie asked.

Evelyn sat down as though she'd been deflated, shaking her head and putting one hand on her cheek.

"It's Francie. She's been snake bit."

"That must be where he was flying to yesterday." Bubba said.

"Oh, no!" A gasp from Tom and a slow whistle from Charlie was followed by an "uh-oh" from Bubba.

"Will she be all right?" Marybelle leaned toward Evelyn, "is Hodges there?"

"Miss Meyers said he's never left her side. He just sits there with his eyes closed.

She says she feels so sorry for him. When he told her he lived up here she thought I might want to know."

"Oh, dear, I recall when they eloped. They were so happy." Marybelle was shocked.

"And I remember," Bubba said, "they were in love when they were kids. All those years."

"And wasn't it sad that they lost those babies?" Evelyn stopped serving the pie. "But they grew even closer."

Marybelle's eyes teared up.

"I'm sure she'll be okay." Evelyn was used to fortifying patients and their families. "I'll keep tabs on them and let you know."

"Do you have any more of that baling twine, Brinksy?" Bubba had been eating with gusto until they heard the news. He hadn't had a home-cooked meal in a while. Now, he wanted to change the subject. "I need your rake, too."

"What are you gonna do, Bubba?" Charlie dug into his pie.

"I thought I'd try to do some planting since I gave up my tobacco allotment. I have to do something in my spare time."

They all laughed.

"So you're gonna borrow everything?" Brinksy kidded him. "You have my plow, Bill Hawkins baler, Walt Hawkins conveyer. I suppose you'll want me to cut and bale it when it's ready?"

"No. I'm gonna ask Roy Palmer to come over from Cosby to do that when it's time." Bubba had all the answers.

"I don't get it, Bubba. When do you have time, with the store and all?" Evelyn was curious. Since Bubba's wife, Mary, had passed away, he worked morning until night at the store.

"Since the days are so long, now, I thought I'd close the store at six and see how much I can get done before dark. Why would I buy anything when I have such generous friends?"

Because there was no crowd, Evelyn and Marybelle got the dishes done and the place cleaned up in no time. Everyone left with Francie and Hodges very much on his mind.

Francie was wide-awake the next afternoon. She opened her eyes to see Hodges slumped over her bed. Her hand reached over and patted his head. He sat up quickly.

"Hodges, you've been here the whole time." Her soft, wonderful voice was back.

"My Darling," he leaned over and kissed her.

"What do they say?" She realized where she was.

"A few more days," he answered, "they want to make sure all the venom and anti-venin are out of your system before they send you home." He held her good hand, kissing it, occasionally.

"Well, then, Sweetheart, why don't you go home, get a shower and take a good rest. You must be exhausted."

"I don't want to leave you." He stood up and stretched.

"It's too bad dear Aunt Blanche passed away. You could have stayed with her."

"Yes. She was a wonderful lady." He again remembered her coming to their rescue.

"Well, I know I'm in good hands, Love, so why don't you go home and rest."

"Only if you promise to rest, too, and get better soon. I'll be back later today." He kissed her goodbye and went to the nurse's station.

The same lady with the pink smock was sitting at the desk.

"How are you, Sir? And how is your wife, today?" She was a sweet old woman, with big splotches of rouge on her cheeks. Her smile was genuine, and he felt she really cared.

"She's doing much better, thank you. I'm going to go home for a little while, and come back later. If there's anything she wants, please see that she gets it."

"Yes, of course. Please wait just a minute." She put her hand up to stop him, and picked up the phone. He thought she had received a phone call, but she called Evelyn, who was back to work, now.

"Hodges!" Evelyn came out of her office, almost running into him and giving him a warm hug.

She continued, "The reports this morning were very good. I peeked in but you were sleeping and I didn't want to wake you, so I asked Miss Meyers to call me when you came out of her room." She could see how happy he was.

"Well, she's awake and talking, so I think everything will be okay. Now, I have to go home and clean up a bit. I'll be back, later." He shook her hand, and gave her a small hug.

He went down the hall, turned the corner toward the parking lot exit, and ran right into Lou.

"Lou," Hodges was surprised. "What's going on? Why are you here?"

"I'll ask you the same question." Lou was his usual surly self.

"Francie was bitten by a copperhead, but she's on the mend, now." Lou could hear the relief in his voice.

"What? When?" Lou was immediately angry with Hodges. He's supposed to protect my Francie, he thought. "Is she okay?" He sounded frantic.

"The worst is over, so I'm gonna jump home for a little bit and come back later. Now, why are you here?"

"I guess you haven't heard. My pa was injured in an accident."

"Hope he does okay." It was the first he'd heard about it.

"If he lives, he'll be here a long time. A truckload of logs fell on him."

"I'm sorry." Hodges realized it was a major incident. "If there's anything I can do, Lou," he put out his hand to shake Lou's.

Lou had an air of annoyance about him, which Hodges took to be anxiety about his pa, but he took Hodges' hand and gave it a perfunctory shake. "Yeah! Thanks!" He started walking towards the Intensive Care Unit.

Hodges watched him go, little knowing he had just added fuel to the fires of anger and hatred Lou had always felt for him. Hodges left.

Lou walked down the hall, then, turned on his heels and crossed to the nurse's desk.

"My neighbor, Mrs. Clark is here. Can I see her?"

Miss Meyers said, "She's in room one fifty-seven." She went back to her paperwork.

Lou went down the hallway and found the room. The door was ajar and he looked in. Francie was asleep again, her one arm still swollen twice its normal size. She looked so little in the big hospital bed it hurt him to look at her, so he turned away and went to sit with his pa.

Sonny was still in a coma and bandaged from head to toe. He had several kinds of tubes attached to him, and Lou could see he had been grossly distorted physically by the accident. His arms and legs were in splints, his body strapped tightly around his ribs.

There was almost no hope for him, in Lou's mind. He sat near the door, trying to decide what to do about the situation, but Francie kept invading his thoughts.

Hodges had no right to let her go into that garden this time of the year. He knows the snakes have come out of hibernation and are likely to be anywhere. What's the matter with him? His mind tumbled over and over. She'd better get well, he stormed internally. What would happen if I lost both Francie and Pa?

He couldn't accept that thought so he rambled on in his mind. I hope she gets well and soon comes to her senses and dumps that ol' mountain man. I wish Lottie would leave like she always promises to. Then, I could go and ask Francie to come away with me and all would be well.

He didn't realize that the shock of the two accidents had him confused. It had always been he and his pa, as long as he could remember. And he'd wanted Francie since they were kids in school, always hoping, that someday, she'd be his. Now, she was in a hospital bed and could have been killed by that snake. If she'd been his from the start he never would have let this happen to her. Lou was becoming more and more obsessed.

He sat with Sonny awhile, and then, got up and walked around the hospital, picking up a cup of coffee from the cafeteria before going back to Sonny's room. He stayed longer than he expected to.

When he looked at his watch he realized he had to get back. The day of the accident he had planned to go to Knoxville for some more supplies but never got there. He knew Rich would be up at the still by now, and wanted to ask him get them, so he told the nurse he'd be back tomorrow, and exited by a side door. He felt it would be too painful to pass Francie's room again.

* * *

The day after she came home from the hospital, Hodges fixed up a bed on the sofa on the screened-in porch for Francie. She was still a little weak in the knees, so he stayed with her in case she needed anything.

All of their friends said that Marybelle's laugh entered a room before she did. And next, her shoes came off. This day, she knocked at the screen door and laughed because she thought they would be in the house, and when Hodges answered right away, it surprised her.

Francie was glad to see her. "Door's open. Come on in."

Hodges stood up and greeted her. Marybelle went over to Francie, leaned down and gave her a hug.

"Well, Kiddo, you sure gave us a scare. How are you feeling?"

Francie rubbed her swollen, bandaged arm. "It's still a bit ouchy but it should heal soon."

"I was elected to tell you what you missed while you were away. Did you hear about Sonny? He'll be in rehab for a while. We had the picnic but it wasn't the greatest. There was nobody there. We vowed to have a better one next year, and you can help us plan it. Let's see. What else?"

It was Francie's turn to laugh. "Slow down, Marybelle, you're like a house on fire."

Marybelle gave her usual chuckle and went on, "I'm trying to remember everything and not leave anything out."

"Oh, Francie, did you know Charlie sold those two acres near Cutter's? He was sure glad to see them go." Marybelle looked far away, thinking of something.

"What is it?" Francie asked.

"That Lou Cutter! I don't know if he's ignorant, stupid, or has a lack of common sense, but he stopped in to Bubba's and told the men not to come up to his place when his pa gets home. Says he'll be in too bad shape to have company. As if any of us would go up there." She looked annoyed.

Francie wasn't sure about the Cutters. She had even told Marybelle at one time that the only time she felt safe around the Cutters was if they were away. She said the middle boy, Billy, had a sneaky look in his eye since he was little. Their Mother was not exactly Stonesthrow material, either, but, mostly, she always felt Lou Cutter looking at her oddly whenever he saw her. She couldn't put her finger on it. She sometimes wished they hadn't lived on adjoining farms.

Marybelle said, "Maybe after he's home awhile Sonny will feel better about his condition. We heard he's bent up pretty badly."

"Maybe. Well, tell Charlie we're happy for him and congratulations on the sale." Francie was enjoying the company. "What else is going on? "

"Well, I got a call from one of my old boyfriends from school, Tyrone Wells. Ol' Ty calls up and asks me to ask Charlie if he wants an ol' coon hound dog that can hunt real good. Now, I know Ty. I know he's up to something. I tell Charlie that dog must be no count, 'cause Ty wouldn't part with anything that's of any count. But you know Charlie, the animal lover. He says 'yeah', so Ty drops the dog off.

"It's a cute dog, all brown and white. Only he can't hear a thing. Deaf as a bucket of rocks. I knew that Ty would have kept it if it was a good hunter. Those puppies are expensive. But Charlie, he don't mind. He's grown attached already, so I guess we have another dog."

With that, Marybelle gave a hearty laugh and they laughed with her. "That's four, altogether."

Francie leaned her head against Hodges' shoulder as he sat on the arm of the couch next to her.

"You must be tired, Dear. I'll go and let you sleep."

"I guess it'll take a little time, Marybelle. Thanks so much for coming by. Please give my love to Charlie and everybody."

When she left, Hodges said to Francie, "I think Sonny will be away a long time. From what I hear he's in bad shape. But what we need right now is for you to get well. And I'm going snake hunting."

"Hodges, that ol' snake might be clear to California by now. Please stay here with me until the sun goes down." She could smell the clean mountain air on his plaid shirt and feel the hardened muscles in his arm.

"Yes, Darlin'," he was so happy to have his beloved Francie home and all right again.

He looked up at the mountain behind their house. He could not imagine Stonesthrow without her. He said a silent prayer of thanks.

In nineteen sixty-eight, Duncan McCloskey, from down in the valley, whose wife, Jen, had passed away a few years before, needed a new suit. Duncan, a small-built man, hard to fit, knew Ada from high school and over the years, he'd heard she could do magic with a sewing machine. He hadn't seen her in a long time, but he knew about Georgie, and about Mrs. Crewe moving in. He knew Jen had gone to Georgie's funeral, and brought her special recipe beans for Ada and the kids, but he'd been busy at the sawmill at the time, and couldn't attend.

He drove to Stonesthrow to see Ada, to hire her to make him a new suit. Ada and Mrs. Crewe were happy to see him. They visited and laughed all afternoon and he never did get measured for that suit.

"I don't mind telling you I haven't had this much fun in a long time." He wiped his bifocals and put them back on. "I've laughed so hard it's brought tears to my eyes.

"You know, Jen and I had all those kids. Now, all six of them are gone. They're all over the country. My Becky, the youngest, married a diplomat. She lives in Japan. We had added on a lot of rooms when they were all growing up. We even put a recreation room in the basement where they could play games and watch TV.

"Now, I just rattle around in that big ol' house and just sit in my parlor at night, listening to soft music, thinking about Jen. Today has been very good for me. Thank you both."

Ada and Mrs. Crewe walked him to his car and after he left, Mrs. Crewe said, "I think that man is courting you."

Ada laughed. That had never occurred to her. "You're mistaken, but it was nice having company."

She put her arm around her mother-in-law as they went back into the house.

Duncan visited often after that, telling them funny stories, making them laugh like they hadn't in a long time. Ada's three children enjoyed hearing about the good old days and they all told their Mother how much they liked Duncan, even though he was an old man. Ada insisted he was young at heart like their Grandma Crewe. She didn't let on how much she enjoyed his company, too.

One night in the late summer, Duncan pulled in the driveway. The moon had risen into a large round ball. The light reflected off his car, parked by the nearby creek. Ada came out to say hello.

"Come on in," she said.

"Oh, can we sit out here a minute. It's such a beautiful night." Duncan took her hand and led her over to a bench she kept near a peach tree. He gazed fondly at her face. She still had the cheerful smile she had as a girl and, although her blond hair showed some gray, she was just as pretty as he remembered.

"Did you notice the flowers this year?" she asked.

"I have a rather large garden at home which I enjoy tending, but this year the wildflowers seem to have outdone themselves." Duncan was nervous. The babbling of the brook muted the sounds of the country and there was a slight breeze.

"What's the matter, Duncan?" Ada was very sympathetic. "You seem sort of upset."

"I am, a little." He wiped his face with his handkerchief and she could see him sweating in the moonlight.

"Dear Ada, I have been enjoying your company all these many visits. It's been very lonely until I began coming up to Stonesthrow. I have that great big house with plenty of room for you and your children. What I'm trying to say is will you marry me?"

His eyes searched hers, looking for the right answer. He almost couldn't believe it when she replied,

"No. Duncan, you have brought us all happy times and we're all very fond of you but marriage would not be possible."

"You don't have to love me. We get along so well. And since Georgie passed away you must be as lonely as I am without Jen." Duncan was becoming frantic. He stood up and went over to lean against his car, wiping his face again.

"What I want you to know, Duncan, is that if things were different I'd be honored to marry you." Ada felt so sorry for him.

"What things?" he stammered. Duncan could not understand what she meant.

Ada got up and stood next to him, casting anxious glances at the house, hoping her mother-in-law wouldn't hear her.

"I would not ordinarily tell you this but the reason we can't marry is Mrs. Crewe. You see, dear Duncan, that lady gave up her own life to help me when Georgie died. She helped me raise my young' uns and I promised I'd always have a home for her. I have no intention of ever breaking that promise." Ada took his hand and held it with both of hers.

"Is that all?" Duncan thought if he were ten years younger he would have jumped up in the air. "Dang!" he swore, shaking his head. "I have plenty of room in that old house. She can come, too." He took Ada in his arms and hugged her.

"In that case, then, the answer is yes." Ada smiled, shyly, and half pulled, half-tugged him into the house to tell Mrs. Crewe.

Mrs. Crewe, who had hoped Ada would marry Duncan, couldn't believe that she'd be moving with them, but she was ecstatic about the turn of events. When he left that evening, she teased Ada, saying," I told you he was a-courting."

Ada just laughed.

As the years ticked by, Lottie's looks faded. She became pencil thin, exaggerating the lines now showing in her face. She tried to cover them with heavy makeup, but Lou never noticed. He went his way and she stayed home, doing as little as possible around the house, watching soap operas most days, and sitting on the porch not speaking, the way his mama did.

Sonny, fueled by anger and hatred, became even more of a bully to her and the boys when he came home from the rehab. It drove him crazy to see a carbon copy of Catherine, and he thought she was just pining away.

Many times, Lou wanted to deliver her back at her daddy's in North Carolina but he knew she wouldn't be welcomed there. He'd taken complete charge of the still and by having occasional mechanic jobs he was seldom home.

Far from feeling sorry for herself, Lottie was plotting her escape. She had planned to leave for a long time. Her problem was pilfering enough money from the moonshine cookie jar. She had to take the tiniest amounts so Lou wouldn't miss it. After awhile, she got tired of hearing herself threaten to leave, and finally, took to just sitting on the porch when she wasn't watching television, not speaking to anyone, even the boys, unless she had to.

At first, she had tried to get along with Lou. He had been a willing pupil as a young lover, but she hadn't planned on marrying him, or living with his pa. The first few years she saw that he was trying to please her. When she was pregnant he took over a lot of her chores, helped her with the babies, and did the cooking and cleaning. He told her he was used to doing it since he was a boy.

He took her to Gatlinburg and bought her pretty clothes, although there was nowhere to go to wear them. They were one of the first on the mountain to have a television although the reception was sporadic. He even took her to a couple of those backwoods country neighborhood picnics, where the women dressed like dowdy old frumps and the men were all hicks.

Her mountain childhood in North Carolina was no better. She had been raised by a stern, unforgiving man, who treated her like a slave. Her mother had died giving birth to another brother, leaving her father with Lottie and her four older brothers. As she grew, he expected her to be the chief cook and bottle washer, often swearing and swinging at her if she displeased him.

Her brothers also treated her mean and had no sympathy for her. They took after their father, as to their attitude towards women. She became sly and sneaky, and constantly thought of leaving someday.

She was fourteen when a traveling salesman stopped by while her family were all away. The man sweet-talked her into doing things she had never heard of, and she found she enjoyed them. He left before her father came home, promising to come back when he was in the area the next time. He never showed up, but there were other salesmen and Lottie soon learned how to please them. They brought her magazines and trinkets, and she enjoyed the challenge of learning new ways to enjoy life, so by the time Lou showed up, she was quite the expert in lovemaking.

She was sorry to turn into what she termed a baby factory and put her foot down that three was all there would be. Eventually, she and Lou began to argue almost constantly, until they wore each other out, and now, they had nothing to say to each other. Lou also couldn't stand the constant wrangling between Lottie and Sonny.

Lottie and Sonny had never gotten along. He was mean-spirited and cold towards her, often seething with rage at her intrusion into the life of him and his son. Her life with her four mountain men brothers and her hot-tempered pa had given her a strong skin for insults and abuse. Sonny didn't frighten her and she gave back as good as she got. Now that he was bent and crippled she hoped neither Lou nor his pa thought she would be his nursemaid. For her own sanity, she had to get away from these people and these blasted mountains and get a life.

It all fell into place the week after Sonny came home from rehab when Walt James dropped by to see Lou.

"How do, Mrs.," he said, as he tipped his broad brimmed hat. "Is Lou in?"

Lottie eyed the tall, thin man, shrewdly. "No, he isn't, and I don't know for sure when he'll be back. His Pa's sleeping." She could tell he would be easily conned.

"I reckon I'll just go see if he's up on the ridge." Walt had no idea she wasn't caring for Sonny. He thought she was a fine lady to be helping her husband's father in his need.

That's mountain folk, she thought to herself, always ready to help, and I was counting on it. To Walt, she said, "My Ma's real sick down to Knoxville and I don't know when Lou will be home, and since his Pa's not well, I'm afraid I'll miss the eight o'clock bus if I don't get down the mountain soon. If you're not in a hurry, could you drop me off at the bus stop in the valley?"

"What a woman," Walt thought. "She has her hands full. Her father-in-law, and now, her ma."

"Of course, I will." He tipped his hat again.

"I packed a few things. I'll just get them." Lottie sounded relieved. As Walt straightened up the front seat of his truck, she went into the house and came out with a small suitcase she had hidden under the bed what seemed like ages ago.

The boys were out behind the barn practicing slingshot shooting and Sonny was sleeping, so she shut the door behind her, got into Walt's truck, and headed for her new life.

"You lyin' snake in the grass!"

Lou's fist shot out faster than a lizard's tongue, catching the man completely off guard. Knocked off balance, his victim fell against the still, gratefully realizing that the fire hadn't been lit under the boiler yet. As Lou came after him again he regained his footing and backed away towards the branch, hands in front of his face to protect himself.

"I swear, Lou, all I did was drive her down the mountain to the bus. If I were up to no good would I come up here? You know me, Walt James, one of your best customers." He kept backing away from the furious moonshiner as he spoke.

"I just stopped in to see if you were to home to get a quart, and she told me her Ma was sick. She said she didn't know when you'd be back, your Pa was asleep and she needed to catch the eight o'clock bus to Knoxville."

"Her Ma's been gone a good many years. She's from North Carolina and her Pa wouldn't have her back there." Lou calmed down a little. "Leave your money on the stump, take your shine and git."

Walt picked up two jars and said, in a timid voice, "I'll see you next week? Sorry, Lou." He practically ran down the rutted logging trail to the pick-up he had hidden in the trees on the other side of the ridge.

Lou went over to the branch and sat on a boulder, feeling as though the breath had been knocked out of him. He watched the little stream as it flowed rapidly from the mountaintop and across the ridge towards the valley below. He stared up at the mountains beyond and tried to sort things out.

If he understood Walt correctly, Lottie was gone for good. She had fooled Walt into believing her Ma was sick down in the valley. If Walt hadn't stopped by how would she have gotten off the mountain? She was stubborn enough to walk if she had to. Walt just happened to be there at the right time. I can picture her packing a small bag and meeting Walt at the end of the driveway before Pa would've known what she was up to. Not that he could have stopped her in his present condition. His thoughts began to tumble around.

"Crafty witch!" He spat that out loud. "And how could she leave the boys? And the youngest just thirteen. Not that she was much of a Ma. Just did what she absolutely had to. Lucky Pa taught me a thing or two about housekeeping and cooking when I was a kid. I hope the boys do okay."

As he sat, he realized the boys were grown enough not to need her anymore. Not that they ever seemed to. They had stayed pretty much in line for the same reason he had—they feared Sonny. He was a strong influence in their lives, for good or bad. They didn't have much use for their moonshiner Daddy, either.

I remember that time I got in trouble at school. Boy, did Pa get after me. His mind went back through the years as he watched the fireflies begin their nightly dance. Made me start working up here at the still, then. I ain't bringing my boys up here, though. I got enough help anyway, with Rich Morris and Jimmie Blake. As Rich says, all you need are two men and a taster.

Lou ran his fingers through his silver-blonde hair. He got up and lit the firewood under the boiler and began stirring the corn he had added. When it was simmering into a mash he sat by the water again. He helped himself to a drink from a mason jar.

"So you finally did it. Never thought you would in spite of all your complaints. I guess you showed me, huh, Lottie?"

Although he drank more than a little he was clear-headed when he got home. Sonny was still up and in his usual seat at the end of the old horsehair sofa reaching down between the arm and the cushion every once in awhile, pulling up a flask, taking a sip, and replacing the container in the couch.

"Well, she's gone." The old man didn't seem to care, either.

"Yeah!" answered Lou. "And that's that."

The next morning Lou drove to Baker's store. Charlie Keene was standing by the front window, drinking coffee, which he almost spilled.

"I'll be," he stammered, "it's Lou."

Before Brinksy had a chance to get to the window, Lou walked in.

"Well, hi, Lou." Bubba had been untying the morning delivery of papers. When Lou came over to him they shook hands. "How're you doing? Ain't seen you in awhile. How's your Pa?"

Lou turned on an angle to include the rest of the men in the conversation.

"My wife had to leave for Knoxville to take care of her aunt. The old lady fell getting out of bed and now, she's an invalid, and there's no one else in the family to help. Don't know when she'll be back. I'm gonna need someone to help Pa with the place, in case you know anyone."

He was taller and younger than any of them and thought he'd pulled the wool over their eyes, but they'd known him too long to start believing him now. He thanked them and left.

"So Lottie's gone," Bubba poured himself a cup of coffee and took a seat. He shrugged. "I'm not surprised. The woman had no life up here."

"Seems to me she left a long time ago." Brinksy had heard Evelyn say that Lottie hadn't been happy there for years, but he didn't know anyone who'd want to go up there and help those Cutter's. Not with Sonny's disposition.

Charlie nodded. "Did you see Lou's squinty eyes? I wouldn't trust him as far as I could throw him. That's why I wanted to sell those two acres and get away from them. They're a bad bunch."

Just then, Hodges came in. He was older than Lou, with a full head of mahogany-colored hair, a tall, well-muscled body and a friendly smile. He looked the same as he always had.

Bubba picked up a small piece of wood from a pile, took a knife from his pocket and whittled as he spoke. "I swan, Hodges, you'll never get old, will you? I reckon Francie keeps you young." He had admired Hodges since he was a boy. "How is that gal of yours?"

"She's fine," Hodges laughed. "She sure does, and right now, she's picking peaches. I just need some fine sandpaper for a picture frame I'm making her for our next anniversary."

"What number is it, Hodge?" Charlie remembered when Hodges eloped with Francie. He and Marybelle agreed that that was a match made in Heaven.

"It's number fifteen, the lucky one. We can hardly believe it. Don't know how that little gal puts up with me." Hodges winked.

"Is it peaches time already?" Charlie said, "They have the best peaches in the county. When did you plant that tree, Hodge?"

"I planted it the week after Francie and I moved in. About a month before my folks went to California." He examined the sandpaper package Bubba gave him and chose the one he wanted, laying the other back on the counter. Bubba put down his whittling and rang up the purchase.

"You've always had a green thumb," he told Hodges. Bubba knew he was a hard worker and his love for the mountain had always been apparent. Besides, he thought to himself, Hodges always went with the Signs that tell you when to plant, and that was why he did so well.

"Just lucky, I guess. Anyway, I'd better get back. Francie's picking them now, and if I know her she'll have a heavy basket before she's done. I'll bring you some." He tipped his cap and left.

"I can't wait. They have enough peaches for the whole county. Marybelle will be making some of her famous peach cobbler, soon." Charlie licked his lips. "I'll bring you some Bubba."

The boys didn't seem to miss their mama much. They never had much use for their moonshiner daddy, either. Sonny had supervised their upbringing, haphazardly, in that they were afraid of him and tried not to get him angry, the same way Lou behaved when he was a boy.

When Sonny came home from rehab they were shocked at his changed appearance and realized he was almost helpless when it came to punishing them. From then on, they went their own way.

Junior was almost seventeen, Billy, almost fifteen, and Jack had just turned thirteen.

Jack enjoyed school. He participated in after-school sports and was usually there on Saturdays. Anything not to have to be home. When he entered junior high just before Lottie left, his guidance counselor told him about an elderly man and his wife in the valley who wanted a youngster to help them take care of their place. He worked hard for Mr. and Mrs. Coleman, and, in time, they asked Lou if Jack could move in with them since it was time consuming and tiring to drive up to Stonesthrow to pick him up and take him home. Lou didn't care, and Jack jumped at the chance. He came to be treated like a son by the Coleman's and never returned home again.

Junior, a carbon copy of Lou, with silver-blond hair, a tall, lean, well-muscled body and the same gray-blue eyes, which changed color with his mood, took a job waiting tables in Gatlinburg when he got out of school. Sonny considered him a traitor because he had expressed a desire to work for the National Park Service as soon as he was old enough. Junior had heard the family story many times as he grew up, but he had also inherited the love and respect for the mountains and wanted to be part of protecting them.

Only Billy, a dark-haired, brooding boy, was sneaky and devious. He had been the toddler who chased and teased the dogs, picked on the chickens, and tormented Sonny as he grew up, always testing his grandpa to see how much he could get away with.

He was in trouble at school quite often and couldn't wait until he was old enough to quit. When he did, he slept late, liked to fish and hunt, and hung out with a boy, Ken, from Cosby, who was older, and had already been in trouble with the law.

One night, he and his friend, Kenny, were cruising around Gatlinburg when Kenny said, "I have an idea."

Billy, who had his feet up on the dashboard, finished his soda, threw the can out of the car window, and sat up straight to listen.

Ken continued, "I'll pretend to have car trouble. You hide in the trees and when one of these rich tourists stops to help me, you come up behind him and knock him on the head. We'll split his money." Ken grinned a nasty grin.

"I was just wondering where I could get some money." Billy liked the idea.

They parked on the side of a quiet back highway. Ken raised his hood and got out and stood by the motor. Billy went down a little embankment and hid behind a tree, a tire iron in his hand.

Eventually, a late model Lincoln, with New York license plates, came by. It stopped a little way in front of the disabled vehicle. The well-dressed man came over to Ken.

"Having trouble, Son?" He was slightly drunk.

He never noticed Billy coming up behind him. Billy hit him with the tire iron and the man fell halfway down the embankment.

"I hope you didn't hit him too hard." Ken was nervous.

"We aren't trying to kill him, just rob him."

"Nah! I just tapped him. Get his pockets."

As Ken cleaned the man's pockets and wallet out, Billy was eyeing the car. Like his daddy and grandpa he had an awe of motors and this was the most beautiful car he'd ever been close to.

"Come on," Ken kept looking down the road, hoping no one would come along. "Let's get away before he wakes up. Here's fifty-two for you." He gave Billy his share.

"You go ahead. I'm gonna take a ride in this neat car." Billy slid into the driver's seat.

"I'm outta here. You're nuts! When that guy comes to you'll be caught." Ken got back in his car and left.

Billy thought the man might be unconscious for a little while so he headed back to Gatlinburg to cruise the streets again, feeling important in his shiny new car. He went up one street and down the other, finally seeing Junior coming out of the cafe he worked at. He blew the horn.

Junior couldn't believe his eyes.

"Where'd you get this car?" He opened the door and got in.

"A friend lent it to me." Billy lied. "Want a ride home?"

"That'd be great. My feet are tired. We were pretty busy tonight."

Junior just sat back to relax on the ride when they heard the sirens. A Tennessee Trooper pulled them over and arrested them both.

Junior was able to convince the judge he had no part in the assault. The judge sentenced Billy to three years in the reformatory and told Junior he could either go there, too, or join the Army. Junior chose the Army, which agreed to wait the three days until his seventeenth birthday. He was stationed at Fort Campbell, Kentucky, making it possible for him to come home on leave often.

* * *

Three weeks after she left, Lottie, who had taken a waitress job at a nightclub in a tough neighborhood in Knoxville, was caught in the crossfire between two brawlers. She was shot in the chest and died immediately. The Sevierville Sheriff notified Lou, who, far from being distressed by it, appreciated the news. Not only was he rid of Lottie and the boys, now he could freely focus on the relationship he still hoped to eventually have with Francie.

Lou Cutter seldom got to Knoxville, but today was important. He hoped to look for a housekeeper to help his Pa, who was finding it harder and harder to get around. He also needed more mason jars for his sideline in the mountains, and buying too many locally, or even in Sevierville, would arouse suspicion. Lou wanted to put a want ad in the paper after he finished his errands. It had been a busy morning and he decided to have a sandwich before finding the newspaper office.

He hadn't been on Cross Street before and was about to turn onto the highway when he noticed Toby's, with its tinted plate glass windows and leaded glass front door. He pulled up and parked.

It was dark inside and he had to adjust his vision as he came in from the bright May sun. He ambled over to the counter and straddled a stool. The place was empty. He looked at his watch. It was almost two-thirty. No wonder he was hungry. The screen door at the back of the building slammed. Leta came in.

"Yes?" She went over to the counter.

It was a little slip of a blonde. She was thin and attractive, but he could see she was wearing too much make-up. He put her age to be about sixteen or seventeen.

"Well, hello Darling!" he smiled, his teeth gleaming white

in the dim light. "I must have died and gone to Heaven, sure enough, 'cause I'm looking at an angel."

"What'll you have?" Leta finally gave him a good look. She could see that he was tall, the way he straddled the stool, with blond hair that looked white in the shaded room, and noticed that he was probably old enough to be her father. She resented being brought out of the reverie of that one happy day in her life, but his smile mesmerized her.

"I'll have a cheese sandwich and a root beer. What's your name?" Lou could turn on the charm when he wanted to.

"Leta." She blushed for staring at him and began to fix his lunch.

"Leta? I never heard that name before." Lou rubbed his fingers through his hair.

"My Mom read it somewhere." It was a short answer. She knew he was flirting with her but she was accustomed to cutting off the wise guys who frequented the cafe every day.

"Ouch! I guess I'm being too nosy?" He pretended to be sorry, but he gave her a big smile.

As she put the frosted mug in front of him she glanced out of the window and saw the red clay of the mountains on his tires. Something clicked in her brain. Maybe that lovely cottage in the mountains wasn't beyond dreaming about. Maybe she could be the one serving lemonade and cookies on the porch.

"Do you live up in the mountains?" Now, she sounded friendlier.

"Yeah! Up on Stonesthrow."

She served his sandwich as she gave him a quizzical look.

"That's the name of our mountain. We're over near Cherokee Ridge." He took a bite of the sandwich.

"Oh, I heard of that. What brings you to Knoxville?"

"I had some errands to run and have to put an ad in the paper for someone to help my Pa around the house. He was injured two years ago, and he's having more and more trouble getting around. By the way, would you happen to know anyone who wants to live up in the mountains?"

She couldn't believe her ears. "I'd like to live up there."

"Would your Ma let you?" He was interested.

Leta gave a dry, hard laugh.

"My Ma doesn't care about me. I've been here since I was sixteen and that's over a year. My stepfather is a drunken brute so I don't spend time at home, only to sleep. My Uncle Toby would hire someone else in a heartbeat. Only he'd have to pay whoever it is much more than he pays me." She started rinsing glasses.

They talked for over an hour. Lou told her about his Pa and his Ma who died from the flu when he was a kid. Little did Leta know his smile was concealing his cunning. He told her how he and his Pa did some logging and tobacco stripping, but he left a few things out. He didn't mention Lottie or the boys, or his sideline business.

"Well, it would be room and board and a small salary. Pa gets around so he doesn't need a nurse. I just need someone to take over the cleaning and cooking for him." He couldn't believe his luck that he found someone so soon. He was thinking of Francie, wondering what she'd say when she heard he had this young girl up there. She'd never know he had no interest in Leta. He hoped she'd be jealous.

She was getting excited that her life was taking this surprising turn. She had always felt she'd live somewhere in the mountains, but didn't expect it to be so soon.

"I'll tell Uncle Toby tonight. Will you pick me up here tomorrow?"

She filled his glass five times until he said, "No more. I'm driving. I'll be back tomorrow around three." He looked at his watch. He put a ten-dollar bill on the counter.

When he stood up she saw that he was over six foot four. His denim jacket showed wide shoulders over slim hips. She thought he was nice looking for an older man. As he left, she started clearing the counter. For the first time in a long time she was hopeful.

The solitary life they had each endured for so long, and their individual desire to use the other for their personal gain had become an unspoken compulsion.

That night, Leta had a huge fight with Uncle Toby. He had been making her work hard with little pay and resented the fact that she would leave him.

"And don't think you can ever come back!" was the last thing he said to her as he gave her her final pay and slammed the cash register drawer shut.

When she got home she took her small stash down from the rafters where she had hidden it, packed a small bag and put it near the door. They were arguing again. She could hear slaps and moans. Bobby was crying into his pillow in the next room. She had no plans to tell them where she was going and just lay in bed in the darkness, smiling.

Lou picked her up in front of Toby's. The ride up the mountain was a surprise. She never imagined the tall ridges and narrow, winding roads would produce a new scene around each curve, of sculptured fields, wildflowers, tiny creeks babbling beneath flimsy wooden bridges which creaked as they drove over them, farmhouses, brick or clapboard, gleaming in the sunshine, and everywhere, men working in the fields, or sitting on their porch, waving, as they passed. The cows, grazing on the slopes, seemed to have two legs shorter on one side. No matter how high they rode, the mountains were always higher.

Leta was enthralled by the views and the lovely scenery reinforced the feeling that she had done the right thing in leaving Knoxville.

"That's our general store," Lou nodded his head in that direction as they passed Baker's. He didn't take his eyes off the road as he turned the corner. "We're just a little further up the road."

He'd been casting furtive glances at her as he drove. She ain't Francie, but she ain't Lottie, either, he thought. Just a slip of a girl, but once that bleach washes out of her hair. Maybe Francie will be jealous to think ol' Lou's got a girl. Well, I ain't telling anyone up there we ain't married. Who's gonna know? Leta won't say. When Francie comes to her senses and dumps Hodges, I'll just take this one back to Knoxville.

Right then and there, he made up his mind that the only Mrs. Lou Cutter there would ever be again would be named Francie. If he had to wait until hell froze over, why, he'd do just that.

They passed the church and parsonage, a few farms, all separated by tall woods, which ran up and behind them to the peaks above, until Lou pulled into a driveway. The grass had taken it over, except for two dull tracks.

"Here we are," he announced, as the truck came to a stop before a large, weathered house.

The Cutter home resembled a wooden cabin on the outside, with a roofed porch that extended all the way across the front. It had been built pre-civil war, a balloon frame, with plumbing and heating added later. The front yard was filled with debris of all sorts. A broken-down chicken wire fence, overgrown with weeds and honeysuckle vines, bordered the road and an open, broken gate leaned against a rotted cedar pole. The whole place looked unkempt and uncared for.

Four big, hungry-looking dogs, all mutts, came out from under the porch. They lay down by the truck with an "I don't care" attitude.

"This here's your new Ma," Lou said, as he came around the truck. "This one's Jake." He kicked at the Shepherd cross who moved lazily away. "This one's Bum. That one's Blackie and the other one's Drifter. They ain't much good for anything but they run the ridges with me and tell me where the snakes are, so I keep them."

She half heard. Looking at the house, she thought, "white clapboard, indeed." The wood was old, withered and gray, with a soot-darkened wall where the pipe from the woodstove came out. The front door was thick and heavy with rusty hinges. The windows were almost too dirty to see in or out of.

He grabbed her suitcase and opened the door. She followed him in.

"We're home," he called.

The first room they came to was kitchen and living room in one. It was a large room and in one corner was a faded red horsehair couch with deep cushions. A little old man sat in the corner of it, bent over. He seemed to be looking at his feet.

"That's Daddy. Pa, this is Leta, your new housekeeper. You can call him Sonny. He doesn't talk much." Lou put her bag down.

Inside, there were several rooms, thanks to the original owners who boarded migrant workers in the summer. Over time, other owners had sheet rocked and wallpapered the rooms and added linoleum, but it hadn't been kept up and it looked shabby. The floors were worn thin with high and low spots.

She almost tripped. There were sturdy wooden chairs at the table so she sat down, at a loss for words. Lou reached up on a shelf above the sink, took down a mason jar filled with white liquid and took a sip.

"Want some?" he offered.

"No thanks." She could hardly think.

When she looked around the room she saw there was a washing machine, refrigerator, and a hot water heater spaced along one wall. The other wall held a sink with a long counter. A cook stove stood on the opposite wall and a wooden table, scratched and worn, was in the center of the room.

There was a doorway at one end leading to the rest of the house and Leta could see a bathroom at the end of the hall. The place wasn't spotless but it wasn't as filthy as she might have expected with two men living there alone. It wouldn't take much to clean it up right. Her faded yellow dress seemed almost as gray as the walls, matching her mood.

"Can I see the rest of the house?" She stood. He took her on a tour.

There were three bedrooms downstairs and four upstairs, all sparsely furnished. Another bathroom was at the top of the stairs. She saw another large room on the first floor, which she thought, might have been a living room at one time but it was empty, now.

"No need to worry about the upstairs. We never use it. I don't go up there and Pa can't. I brought one of the beds down for you and put it in the back room." As they walked through the rooms, she was relieved to realize he had no designs on her. At least, not yet.

When they returned to the kitchen they both sat down at the table. Lou had another drink as he watched his Pa, using a cane that he picked up from the floor as a crutch and the arm of the couch to brace himself, get up and limp outside. He slammed the front door and Leta jumped.

Lou noticed. He told Leta, "I don't want you going to Baker's store by yourself. You might slip and tell someone you're single. There's a strict code in these hills and they'd like to tar and feather you if they thought you were living up here with my Pa and me without being married. It'd be easier for all of us if you just let them think we were. Do you have anything to say?"

She seemed to have left her big city smart mouth back at Toby's. Her romantic notions about starting a new life were turning into major fears. Fear that she really didn't know this tall mountaineer sitting across the table from her in this dingy house high up on the side of a mountain.

She was also afraid that if his neighbors knew she was up here with this man and his father without a wedding ring they would consider her a Jezebel, and there was no telling what they'd do to her then. There was a bone-chilling fear that now that she had taken this step there was no turning back. No one knew or cared where she was. There was nowhere else to go. The biggest fear of all was that if she didn't please this stranger he might turn her out and what would become of her?

He was saying something.

"I asked if you had anything to say?" He took another gulp from the jar.

She walked over to the window to peer out at the small clearing the house was on. She could see that dark woods, which reached above, higher than she could see, surrounded the place.

"Do you farm?" She tried to sound confident.

"Nah! I get by." He was starting to feel the moonshine. "I rent my tobacco allotment. We get by." He laughed then, not the warm, friendly laugh she had heard in Knoxville, but a cold, hard laugh she couldn't decipher. She felt a chill.

"Can I fix you some supper?" She rubbed her arms with her hands and walked over to the refrigerator. "There are some eggs."

"That'll be fine."

"I don't cook much more than fast foods but I am willing to learn."

He thought about Francie again. She was a great cook. Her dishes and baked goods were the talk of the mountain and the valley below. He had done the family cooking since he was a boy, and even when Lottie was there, so he wasn't too worried about that. Maybe Leta would learn in time.

When the eggs were ready he called his Pa in. Leta finally got a good look at him as he hobbled to the table.

He wore dirty brown pants that were much too big for him. The cuffs were rolled up almost to his knees and she realized he had been a lot taller at one time. A worn leather belt was wrapped around his waist, with one end hanging loose. His dirty blue shirt also looked made for a much larger man. The worn felt hat he dropped on the couch as he came in was full of lint and dog hair.

His gray hair was thick, long and uncombed. His sallow skin emphasized his beady brown eyes, which were hard to see because he was so bent over that his chin almost touched his chest. His arms were as thin as parchment paper and his hands were gnarled and twisted, with dirty fingernails.

He sat at the table without a word, head down, eyes roaming back and forth over his plate as though he were looking for some hidden item in his food. He chewed noisily and grunted between forkfuls. His crippled body looked as though it might slide off the chair and under the table any minute.

Some of his food dribbled onto his chest. When he was through eating, he rubbed the particles of food off his shirt with the backs of his wrists, leaving stains in their wake.

He was acutely aware of Leta watching him. Sonny hated his loss of independence and the inability to control his movements. He also hated Leta for intruding and his anger extended to Lou for bringing her there.

When he left the table he got up slowly, and made his way back to the couch, and sank down in the corner where he'd been when they came in. He watched her clear the table, as he reached down between the arm of the couch and the cushion and pulled up a small flask. He opened it and took a good swallow before replacing the flask in its hiding place.

"That's his painkiller." Lou laughed. "Ain't nothing better. I'm going out."

"Where are you going?" She was bewildered to think he'd leave her all alone the first night she got there, especially with this crusty old man.

"I got something to take care of. We might as well get this straight right now. I have a life up here that's nobody's business, including yours, so don't ask me. I'll be back when I get here. Make yourself to home." He put on a cap and left.

Leta stood there, staring at the door. She had recoiled at his change of heart. It had frightened her enough to know she'd better do as he said. She looked at the old man who was smirking into his chest. He seemed to enjoy her discomfort.

When the dishes were done she went out onto the porch. There was an old cane rocker there, its seat broken in some places, the cane winding in all directions. She bent some of the wood back far enough to have a seat and tried to think.

The fireflies began chasing each other in the early evening dusk. The mist was rising from the valley, causing an enchanting fog to cover the land. Lou had told her in Knoxville the Cherokees called it Sha-co-na-ge, The Land of Blue Smoke.

Leta thought that being here in a friendless loneliness was better than the home life she had left. She had loved the mountains all of her life. Now she had them. She resolved to try to make the best of the situation, come what may.

When she realized that Sonny had turned a lamp on she went inside. He had gone to his room so she went to hers, falling asleep almost as soon as her head hit the pillow.

It took her about two weeks to get the pattern of day-to-day life at the Cutter home. Sonny only spoke to her when it was absolutely necessary, and then in a gruff tone. She noticed that Lou came in around eleven at night, carrying a mason jar with whiskey in it. He'd sit at the table and take a few sips, getting tipsier by the minute.

Sometimes, he'd talk aloud to himself, usually mumbling incoherently, and other times she could hear phrases and curses as she lay in bed. One night he'd curse the moonshiners for not making the liquid strong enough and the next, it would be too strong. She also heard him talking about

Francie, but she had no idea who that was. One particular night, he seemed happy with the jar contents so she knew she'd be able to talk to him the next morning.

He was still in bed when she got up to start breakfast. When he came into the kitchen she was cooking. She wasn't as full-figured as Lottie, nor as eye pleasing curvy like Francie. From the back she was as thin as a boy.

"What's for breakfast? Where's Pa?" He seemed more like the Lou she'd met. She felt a little braver than she had. "Some man drove by to pick up your Pa. Said his name was Rich. I have a question for you."

"What's that?" He was wary.

"Your Pa won't talk to me and you're gone so much. There's a little television upstairs. Would it be all right if I use it?"

"The reception isn't that great up here but you're welcome to." He was relieved to hear the question.

"I'm going crazy trying to find things to do now that I have the cleaning and the laundry caught up."

"Well, you wanted to live in the mountains, didn't you? And I wanted someone here to look after things so the nosy neighbors wouldn't be trying to help Daddy. And then, there's the boys." His eyes narrowed, as he laughed out loud.

"Boys? What boys?" She was dumbfounded.

"Oh, didn't I tell you? You're a step-mama, now." His smile was cruel. She realized he hadn't been cool, he'd been slick. "You have three sons, sort of." That gave him a hearty laugh as he watched her face change from shock to disbelief.

"I don't believe you." She looked at him sideways, chin tilted. "Where are they?"

"Junior's in the Army, Billy's in jail and Jack lives down in the valley. They aren't coming home anytime soon. You don't have to worry about them." The joke over, he started to eat his eggs. His eyes were a bright blue, now, and she knew he had pulled a real swindle on her.

Leta shuddered. "Where's their Mama?" She felt as though she'd been punched in the stomach.

"She's long gone." He didn't seem too distressed. "She got shot and killed in a bar fight over to Knoxville awhile back."

Leta remembered hearing something about a waitress getting shot when she had the news on at Toby's. She sat down, feeling very deflated.

"I'm sorry, Lou." She didn't know what else to say.

"She'd left us a long time before that," he said, "so by the time that happened we had really lost track of her. Poor Lottie. She never knew what she wanted out of life. Knew it wasn't me or the boys, though." Lou didn't sound remorseful or sad. He acted as though he were talking about a complete stranger. He left after he had eaten.

Leta moved as if she were in a trance the rest of the day, doing the chores in a foggy haze. She tried to picture Lou and Lottie, with their three little boys and his Pa before he got hurt. They could have been so happy but they seemed to be just as sorry a family as the one she had left in Knoxville. The idea that probably no one is ever really happy or satisfied, depressed her.

Late in the afternoon, before it was time to fix supper, she went out back and looked up at the tall ridge behind the house. She wanted to go up there and jump off, but Lou had told her about rattlesnakes and bears, so she just sat on a pile of old boards behind the barn until Sonny's friend dropped him off. Again, Sonny wouldn't talk to her but took his seat on the old couch. Lou came in soon and they ate in silence, each lost to his own thoughts.

The empty days and lonely nights wore the same face. Leta tried to make the place look a little better. One day, she tried to rake the front yard, but the dogs kept dragging more debris and depositing it there, so she gave up. They were mean-tempered, mangy and ugly, so any idea she had of playing with them was soon stifled.

She would sit by the hen house for a long time watching the chickens forage for grubs. She got a big kick out of hearing them squawk when the rooster chased them and they'd run away, making her think of little old ladies running while holding their skirts up.

She didn't mind feeding them but she had to watch all the time to keep the dogs away from them. Every once in awhile, a dog would slip into the hen house, cause a flurry of excitement, and before she could chase him out, he'd stolen an egg.

After supper, Lou would leave, coming home late. He'd sit at the table and drink from his jar. Sometimes he'd curse at the ineptitude of the men he had working for him. She figured out he was in the moonshine business but would never bring it up to him.

If he had a good run he was considerably nicer to her the next day. If not, she'd stay out of his way, speaking only when she was spoken to, losing her grip more and more on the life she thought she would have up there and now knew was never going to happen.

Some days, Lou would announce he was going to town. She knew he meant Knoxville and once asked if she might go along.

"No," he answered, "you'd better stay here in case we have any visitors." That idea was so preposterous to him he threw back his head and laughed. His eyes began to water from laughing and as he wiped them she could see they were a cold, flat gray instead of a a bright blue.

Leta had learned to determine his mood by the shade of his eyes. She thought he might be angry but she asked him, anyway.

"When you get the groceries could you pick up a movie magazine for me?"

"Not on your life. There's no way I'd be seen buying that trash." He remembered that Lottie used to read them and always thought that's where she got all of her high-falutin ideas.

She blinked back tears. He was angry again. It seemed to be easier and easier to annoy him. He slammed out of the house, revved the engine and peeled out of the driveway.

She was afraid to open the door and watch him leave, but went into her room, sat on the bed and began to cry. Where were the high hopes she had coming up here?

"If Uncle Toby could see me now he'd take me back," she day-dreamed, knowing that the truth was he only wanted her to work in the cafe and had no affection for her, either.

Sobbing aloud, she asked, "Is there no one for me in this whole world?" Alarmed, Leta turned her head to make sure no one heard her. She knew no one was there. No one was ever there. And no one ever would be there. She started to cry again, loud, long sobs of self-pity and defiance.

Sonny heard her and he smiled. Good, he thought, maybe she'll go back where she came from.

One afternoon, when both Lou and Sonny were out, she decided to take a walk down the steep road. She picked her way through the trash-strewn yard, shouting at the dogs not to follow her. They weren't interested. Bum snarled at her from under the porch, while the others lay in various spots, too lazy to get up.

The farms were spaced far apart and she had no way of knowing that the farm across the road belonged to the Crewe family. Since Carol and Bud had moved back to the valley because his job as an appliance repairman meant he had to be mobile and the roads were almost impassible up there in the winter, and Ada and Mrs. Crewe had moved in with Duncan, the property was for sale.

Leta saw that the place was deserted. The grass needed to be mowed and the house was empty, which added to her sense of absolute isolation. It was as empty as her soul seemed to be. Frustrated, she turned around and went back.

When he returned, Lou brought her three new dresses. He'd guessed the size pretty well so they weren't too big but they emphasized how thin she was.

"Gad, girl! We have to get some meat on your bones." He was in a very good mood. His eyes were a bright blue and she guessed he either had a good batch of moonshine the night before or something good had happened in Knoxville.

After Lou left for the evening, Leta sat on the old broken rocker on the porch until it got dark. The humidity had become almost oppressive. About nine o'clock, the rain finally started, a slow steady rain, running down from the ridge in rivulets which wound around the debris in the yard and made deep puddles in the driveway ruts causing the clay underneath to turn into gooey, sodden clumps. The roof of the porch sheltered her for a long time until the thunder and lightening began. She went inside and sat at the table. The old man had gone to bed. Thunder tore loose from the mountain tops and the dazzling lightening displays crackled behind the house but she was too nervous to get closer to the windows in case the glass broke.

She moved her chair nearer to the wall, and began to cry, a low, moaning sound. The loneliness was hard enough to bear but being alone in a terrifying thunderstorm was giving her second thoughts about coming to the mountains. At Toby's, she never gave a thought to a storm, except for mopping the floor after the customers came in from the rain.

Sharp cracks directly overhead made her duck and close her eyes. She gave a slight scream when the door opened. The lightening illuminated Lou, standing in the doorway, soaking wet. She had to stop herself from running to the safety of his arms. He was grinning and he smelled of "shine."

"Scared ya, did it?" He didn't look at her, but sat down at the table with a jar in his hand. "Just a little ol' storm." He sounded matter of fact until he said, angrily, "Couldn't even finish a batch. And it was coming good until the rain started and put the fire out. Now, we have to start all over." He peeled off his wet shirt and dropped it on the floor.

"I'm going to bed." She watched, as he staggered to his room.

The storm had subsided. The thunder was moving fast over the mountains and the rain reverted to the slow steady rain it had been earlier. Leta picked up the shirt, hung it over the back of a chair and went to bed.

During the second week of June, Junior was granted a thirty-day leave before being deployed to Germany for two years. He planned to spend two weeks on Stonesthrow and two weeks with one of his army buddies in New York State to help celebrate his friend's parents' twenty-fifth anniversary. Junior was unfamiliar with a normal home life and was looking forward to the party.

No one was home but he knew his Pa and Grandpa would be there soon. He put his duffle bag in his old room took an apple from a bowl on the kitchen table and went out the back door. He wanted to climb the ridge one more time.

There was a young woman sitting on an old bench near the hen house. She seemed to be daydreaming. He stood there a minute, just watching. She was a waif of a girl, young and thin, and he knew she was the girl who came to do the housework and help Grandpa.

"Y'all look like a scared li'l rabbit." He had a big smile on his face.

She jumped at the sound of his voice and turned to see Lou standing there. But it wasn't Lou. This man wore a uniform, and although he was half-hidden by the willow tree bordering the path, he lacked the hard, cynical lines she'd come to know so well. The sun shone on him and she knew, as she knew her own name that love had come to her at last.

"You must be the little gal Pa brought up here to help Grandpa. I'm Junior."

She shielded her eyes from the sun. He caught the glimmer in them before she blushed and lowered them.

"I'm Leta," she said.

"So you're my new Ma." he tried to kid but realized the remark fell flat. She kept staring at her feet and looked as though she might faint. He threw the apple down.

He was at her side and caught her, taking her in his arms to keep her from falling off the bench. He was quickly aware of how thin she was through the faded cotton dress she wore. He lifted her chin and she opened her eyes. They were green, swimming with unshed tears. She looked into his, seeing her whole life in his gaze. Still in shock from the sight of him, she was aware of the muscles of his chest and arms as he held her tightly.

"Don't cry. I was just teasing. I'm on leave for two weeks before I get shipped out to Germany. I knew you were up here but I had no idea you were younger than I am."

Leta was comfortable with his arm around her shoulder. She felt giddy and weepy, foolish and happy, all at once.

"I'm okay, now." She smiled at him, the biggest, and maybe the only smile, she gave since she came here.

"Let's go out behind the barn. If nosy ol' Grandpa comes home he won't be able to see us there." He stood up and took her hand and led her behind the tobacco barn, where they sat on a huge, old stump.

Her bravado returned as she gave him a long look.

"I keep getting all of these surprises. I just heard about you and your brothers the other day."

"Yeah, Billy." He sneered. He took both of her hands.

"How'd you get up here?"

She finished her tale quickly, looking at his wonderful face the whole time. He learned she would be eighteen the end of September and that his Pa had told her he'd marry her then. Neither of them knew Lou had lied.

133

"I have no choice," she told him. "I have nowhere else to go, and I'm always worried that Lou will turn me out."

His heart was touched by the poor girl's history and he suddenly felt the need to protect her. He surprised himself. His feelings were quickly matching hers. So this was what "Love at first sight" was like. Aloud, he promised her that he'd see to it that she had better prospects than becoming an old man's housekeeper with no life of her own.

"Pa's away at night and Grandpa goes to bed early so meet me at the hay barn around ten o'clock. I'll try to see a way around this situation."

They returned to the hen house and he watched her feed the chickens. She saw nothing but his perfect face, as she dropped the feed pan before she was through, almost tripped over a chicken, pinched her finger as she locked the gate, never feeling it, and left the lid off the feed box, until Junior went over and closed it.

A truck pulled into the driveway. It was Rich Morris bringing Sonny home. Junior went out to meet them.

Leta felt that she was floating up to the house, sobering up only when she reached the back door, fully aware that the old codger would be watching her every move and would report her to Lou if he noticed anything different. She had never been so happy in her young life and found it hard not to hum a tune as she prepared supper.

She sat on the porch that night until Sonny went to bed. Lou had to go up on the ridge and invited Junior but he declined, saying he was tired from the trip.

At ten, Leta joined him in the hay barn. She had been waiting for him all of her life and walked right into his arms. He showered her face with soft, tender kisses, her eyes, her nose, her ears, and when he nuzzled her neck he could feel her tremble. She was such a frail, fragile wisp of a girl; he handled her carefully, as though she might break.

She was lost in his loving and gave herself willingly, totally. The love-starved girl opened up like water spilling over a dam, her pent-up emotions pouring from her heart. She surrendered completely to the only person in her life who'd been kind to her. The moments were magical, transcending time and space.

Afterward, they sat quietly in the hay, not wanting to break the spell. He finally spoke.

"I am being sent away for two years, Leta. Will you wait for me?" To him, she seemed like a fragile sparrow, ready to fly at a moment's notice.

She was too wrapped in a rosy glow to realize what he was asking her at first.

She then told him about Uncle Toby and that she knew he would never take her back. Now he realized why she had seemed so anxious and concerned.

"When is your birthday?" he asked, putting his arm around her shoulder and holding her close. She smelled the hay on him and nestled her head into his shoulder.

"In September."

"I'll have some money saved by then and I will send you enough for a bus ticket to anywhere you want to go. You can get a job there and wait for me. When I get back we'll get married."

His sincerity touched her heart and she looked up at him. The moon was behind a cloud and the barn grew darker. The shadows on his face made him look young and vulnerable. She reached up and touched his cheek.

"I won't send the money here. I'll ask Mr. Baker, down at the store to keep in touch with me and I'll ask him to get it to you." He set his jaw. "Now, we'd better get back to the house. Grandpa only takes catnaps, and Pa may be home soon."

The glow in her cheeks would have certainly made the old man suspicious but he had gone to bed sometime earlier. Lou wasn't back from the still yet. Leta went to her room and got ready for bed while Junior got into the car he'd borrowed and drove down to the valley to spend the night with his brother, Jack.

She sat in the dark most of the night. His image began to fade in the dawn's first light. She thought it would be a long time before they would be together again and her heart began to slowly break. To have finally found love and have to let it go so quickly! She had been alone all of her life, and now, that she had someone, she never felt so lonely.

She could hardly believe that Junior felt the same way that she did. He came up to Stonesthrow every day to see her. He'd wait until Sonny and Lou would go on their errands and take Leta into the barn and make love to her. Each time, the two lonely people felt the earth move, the life force flow into them, and the incomparable joy of becoming one.

Two days before he was to leave, Junior invited Leta to take a walk up to the top of the ridge. It was almost July, warm, but not too humid. She had a few hours until supper time. Lou had told her he'd be later than usual, and Sonny was gone again.

Junior took a pistol from the kitchen cabinet. Her eyes got wide.

"In case we see a snake," he explained.

She followed him out behind the dilapidated barn and they started up the ridge. The dogs tried to follow but Junior kicked at the one called Drifter, who ran, howling, back under the porch, even though the heavy boot hadn't touched him. The others decided not to go along.

The climb was steep. By the time they reached the top they were both breathless.

The view was stunning. All around them, the mountains seemed endless. The ridges between each mountain pointed like fingers toward the unattainable summits. On and on, the scene went, toward the distant horizon, a smoky blue haze beginning to form in the valleys below.

Leta was awestruck. The clearing they were in had been logged years ago and the saplings were too young to reclaim it, but the wildflowers were a mass of colorful beauty. She could never have imagined such a lovely place.

Junior stood over near the edge. He pointed to a neighboring mountaintop.

"Over yonder's where my grandpa came from. That's called Cherokee Ridge. His family goes back three generations, there, until he moved to Stonesthrow." He waved his hand in that direction.

She seemed puzzled.

"All of these ridges have nick-names from the folks who live on them. Everyone calls our ridge, "Stonesthrow", because, the land is so rocky, every year before they can till the soil, the farmers have to pick all the rocks and pebbles out of the dirt and pitch them so they can plow. It never quits.

"If you go up a little further on that ridge over there," he pointed to a chain link fence she could barely make out on the opposite mountain, that's the National Park. My great-great-granddaddy lived just below there with the Cherokee Indians a long time ago. He came from Scotland, all by himself when he was fifteen."

"Tell me," she begged, as she sat down on the grass. He joined her, his hand roaming gently over her cheek, her arm and her hand.

"He was actually English. When he was little, his parents took him to Scotland. They died in a house fire when he was fourteen. He walked to Edinburgh where he signed on a ship as a cabin boy in return for a trip to America. It was around eighteen forty-six.

"When he arrived in this country he tried to work on the docks, loading ships. But he was still just a boy and there was one sailor in particular who didn't like him or his Scottish brogue. One night, the man got drunk and came at him with a baling hook. He got him right in the eye. The other sailors rescued Robert, that was his name, and he recovered, but they couldn't save his eye, so he wore a patch on it from then on.

" He decided to find another line of work, and arrived in north Georgia right after the gold rush there had petered out, and the prospectors left for California. He kept moving closer to the mountaintops in Georgia, but there were frequent Indian uprisings and marauding white troublemakers, so he crossed the border into Tennessee.

"He met a trapper who took him under his wing and taught him everything he knew. Along the way, the man introduced him to some of his Cherokee friends who still lived up there. They'd been taken advantage by the white man over and over but they trusted Robert. Maybe they felt sorry for him because he'd come so far at such a young age and had only one eye, or they admired his gumption. They called him Di-ta-li, for "One-eye."

"Whatever the reason, they gave him a plot of land and helped him build a cabin and my family lived there until my Pa was about two years old.

"In nineteen thirty-four, the National Park Service took over the mountain tops. The government had taken the land from the Cherokees and gave it to the states long before, so there were just a few private farms up there. The rest of the land belonged mostly to lumber companies same as the one at the top of Stonesthrow road. EP's had that one since way before I was born. I doubt they'll ever log up there, or over on Cherokee Ridge, either."

They shared a few light kisses before he went on.

"We didn't actually own the land so my Grandpa had to go. He had no formal education, other than learning to read and write, somewhat, and not enough money to fight for the land. Wouldn't have won, anyway.

"He found the fifty acres we have now, on Stonesthrow and waits for the day we can move back up there. He talks all the time about how we were cheated and how the park caused his wife and three babies to die early. He complains that it brings all kinds of tourists to our peaceful region. I've heard it all my life. Unfortunately, I used to work in Gatlinburg and I often toured the park. It's in my blood and Grandpa calls me a traitor because I mentioned that I wouldn't mind becoming a park ranger someday, to help protect the area.

"When I was little, if he sampled a bad batch of corn liquor they make up on the ridge behind this one, he'd get fighting mad about the park again, and smack us around. He'd kick the dogs and scream and yell until he got out of breath and swear about the injustice of it all. He hated my Mama and she, likewise, hated him. Those two were always at it."

She stood up and walked over to the opposite side of the ridge. When he joined her he said, "That land down there belongs to Hodges Clark and his wife. He had some land when his Daddy went to California, and when his wife's father moved to Oklahoma he gave him that ridge over there, so they have about sixty acres. My Pa has always hated the Clark's. I don't know why."

"Was your Grandpa a trapper, too?" She stood with his arm around her, feeling safe and secure.

"He was, until he moved here. Then, he did day work, logging or tobacco work, until he got hurt."

"What happened?" She was interested in Sonny's accident.

"The braces on a truck of logs snapped and some of the logs rolled off and buried him just as he walked past the side of the truck. He was almost killed. Odd, isn't it? He was also about as tall as me and Pa, and look at him now." He shook his head. "I can't imagine how he lived through it. Guess he's too ornery to die. We'd better go now."

Coming down the ridge, he had to hold her hand and guide her through the trees. He was used to the rocky terrain, but she almost tumbled a few times.

When they reached the farmyard, Leta went to feed the chickens and Junior went back down to the valley to see Jack again.

The day before he left for good he met her at the hen house. He promised to send her the money to get away, and told her that he loved her and would be back for her. They hugged and kissed goodbye. Neither of them knew that Sonny had been in the 'bacca barn getting a bucket for the still and overheard them. He waited until they were out of sight until he went back into the house.

Leta had been so glad to have one more clandestine meeting with Junior that she felt she could now let him go away and await his return with love and joy in her soul.

When he left, Sonny and Lou shook his hand and wished him luck. Leta stayed in the house and looked out of the window. She didn't want to seem too interested. They had said their goodbyes the night before.

One day followed the next that summer. There was plenty of day work for Lou. The tractors and hay balers were all doing double duty so there was a lot of mechanical repair needed. Sonny went out at least one day a week with his friend, Rich Morris, and Leta tried to do her chores. She thought of Junior every waking moment and it sustained her.

Lou noticed there had been a change in her but couldn't put his finger on it. Sonny noticed, too, but he knew what it was and it infuriated him. He was determined to fix that once and for all.

In the middle of September, the week before Leta's birthday, she woke up nauseous. She knew, immediately, what was wrong, and was beside herself. For a brief moment she was delighted to think she'd have a smaller version of her lover to keep until his return, but she realized the horrible implications of it. She knew she couldn't stay on Stonesthrow, but where? And how could she bring up a child by herself?

She thought that if she could get word to Bubba Baker he might be able to reach Junior and tell him about this turn of events. She remembered Lou's admonition the first day she arrived that the neighbors might tar and feather her if they knew she lived there, unmarried. What would they do to her if they discovered she was pregnant?

She could never return to Knoxville, nor would she want to. There was nowhere for her to go. And she would not bring up a child in the loveless world she was raised in. Still, she tried to find a glimmer of hope.

Sonny had kept his beady little eyes on her and he knew the signs. Now it was time for the axe to fall. He'd get her out of his hair once and for all.

The next morning, when he knew she was within earshot, but not in the room, he said to Lou "Bubba got a letter from Junior."

Slowly and distinctly, he said, "Junior says he really likes Germany and that he's met a cute little gal there. He says it's pretty serious and when his hitch is over he may just marry her and live there."

The words rolled off his tongue cutting Leta sharper than any knife in the world could. He spit it out with contempt in his voice, making sure she heard every word.

She panicked, and tried to pretend she hadn't overheard. All of the Cutter's are the same, she thought. What a fool I've been.

The rest of the day passed in a haze. She felt trapped like an animal and she imagined that Sonny, the old trapper, wanted her to feel that way. The poor girl stayed in her room all day. When she fixed their supper she told Lou she couldn't eat because she felt she was coming down with something. Sonny just snarled into his food. Lou had no clue as to what was going on.

In the morning her mind was made up. After Lou left for Knoxville and Sonny went off with Rich, Leta walked down the driveway. This time, she didn't stop at road's edge. She headed straight down the winding road towards Bubba Baker's general store. She had no intention of going inside to ask about Junior. Sonny had made Junior's plans very plain.

It was almost a mile to Bubba's and the county highway. Leta hoped she wouldn't run into anyone. She made it across the highway and turned sharply to the right. She headed west for a while when a large furniture truck came up behind her. The driver was surprised to see this waif of a young woman with her thumb up but he stopped, anyway.

"How far are you going?" he asked, as she climbed into the cab.

"Just over the river bridge," she lied. "My Mom lives over there and she's not feeling too well today." She looked straight ahead.

"Name's Jim," he said, "what's yours?"

"Leta," she said it so softly he thought she said Rita.

"Well, Rita, it's a little cool to be out today, isn't it? This is a pretty nice area up here. I just delivered a chair to the Brinks. Do you know them?"

She didn't answer so he gave up trying to have a conversation.

In no time at all, they reached the far side of the bridge. There was a long gravel driveway leading to a farmhouse set way back from the road.

"This is it," she said. She had figured on having him stop at the first farm they came to.

He pulled the big rig to a stop on the side of the road and asked, "Will you be all right?" He was almost reluctant to leave her out here all by herself.

Leta climbed down and pretended to walk up the gravel road. The trucker started driving but could not resist watching her in his rearview mirror for a minute. She seemed so sad. He drove a little way and looked back again.

He saw her turn and head for the bridge. She almost ran towards the center as he watched with horror, suddenly realizing what she was about to do. He pulled back to the side of the road, turned off the engine, jumped down from the cab and started running. He was too far away to help.

Without any hesitation, Leta climbed over the railing and jumped, one hundred and thirty feet into the Little Pigeon River.

Earlier that same morning, Lou said, "I'm going to Knoxville for some corn."

Sonny answered, "Rich is taking me up on the ridge. I'll spend the day there because Rich has to run down the mountain for something."

Lou watched the old man pick up his hat with much difficulty and was glad the girl was there to do the chores. He felt all day would be too hard on Sonny, so he said, "Then tell Rich he won't have to come back. I'll stop up and pick you up when I get back. Where's Leta?"

Sonny scowled, "She's still in her room, I guess. I wish you'd never brought her up here." He stamped the floor with his cane, for emphasis, and hobbled out onto the porch.

The mountain air was cool and crisp, bringing the clarity of the surrounding foliage colors to a spectacular intensity. It surprised Lou when Sonny, in an unexpectedly mellow voice, said, "I always liked Fall best." and he was even more surprised to hear that his cranky, stern old father ever liked anything.

He didn't know what to say to that, so he changed the subject. "Leta must be sick. I'll let her sleep and check on her when I get back."

Lou watched Sonny climb into Rich's truck. He saw that his Pa was in a lot of pain and it was a job for him to get situated. When they had left, he got into his truck and drove away.

Rich drove down to the county highway towards Gatlinburg, and took a little known side road that led up to the back of Cutter's ridge. He soon turned onto a rutted, narrow wagon trail used for logging years before. The road was rough and steep and the trip was hard on Sonny, who felt every bump.

"I heard at Bubba's that Junior went to Germany. Have you heard from him?" Rich started the conversation.

"No," Sonny was emphatic. "And I told that little gal that Lou brought home that he's never coming back."

Rich didn't see the evil twinkle in the old man's eyes.

"I seen the both of them making out behind the barn. They didn't know I was there. She thinks he's coming back for her so I set her straight. I want her to go away. Faraway. Me and Lou, we don't need that gal up here."

When they reached the top of the ridge Sonny sat in the truck a minute, opening the window as he inhaled the fragrance of the mountains. He drank in the splendor of the rugged peaks all around him. It reminded him of the property he had once owned on Cherokee Ridge, where he sat on the porch on warm evenings to watch the sunsets, and enjoyed the vast view across the ridges, feeling safe and secure from intruders. He thought that he'd never let go of Cherokee Ridge and the life of a trapper, but he'd come to love Stonesthrow almost as much.

He told Rich, "You won't have to come back for me. Lou said he'll pick me up when he gets home from Knoxville."

Rich chuckled, "Ol' Lou may get stuck over there with one of those fancy gals. Tell you the truth, I thought he might have some ideas about that gal."

Sonny said, vehemently, "No! She's just a dumb kid. And after Lottie left he told me he never wants to get married again. He gets all the gals he wants in Knoxville."

"Smart move," Rich agreed. "Okay! See you tomorrow." He backed out of the trees and left.

Sonny's resentment flourished as he replayed his hard luck existence in his mind. He held the United States Government responsible. He blamed them for the loss of his wife and three dead babies, Lou's ne'er do well kids, his crippling accident. He felt it had all begun when he was evicted from his little patch of Paradise, which had been home to the Cutter family for generations.

His daddy had told him the story of his grandpa and how he'd come all the way across the ocean to settle in this beautiful place. He was grateful to the mountains for the abundance of pelts he used to sell. And there was lovely Catherine. And Rosemarie, his dear little sister and playmate of so long ago, who had died, tragically, at only twelve years of age of Pneumonia, after she got the measles. He hadn't thought of Rosemarie in a long time.

Sonny, always fiercely independent, had determined that the results of his accident were not going to incapacitate him any more than it absolutely had to, devised a way to get around, bent over as his crippled spine would allow, hating and cursing his every waking moment, either inwardly or vocally.

All of these things were on Sonny's mind as he got out of the truck. Sonny slowly made his way down the ridge, holding on to the trees and using his cane where he had to, to help ease the momentum. He rinsed a few jars in the creek and thought he heard a twig snap. He looked around. Everything seemed to be all right. He emptied some of the distillate into five jars which he lined up behind the boiler to be poured into the next batch when Lou fired up the still again.

There was another noise.

As an old trapper and mountain man, Sonny knew there was movement in the woods. He started up the ridge. His physical condition prohibited speed and he had just gotten a few yards up when a shot rang out. He rolled behind a tree.

The tax men came out of the trees below him, used their rifles to smash everything, knocked over the boiler and dumped the last tub. Satisfied that the still was inoperable, they left the way they had come, heading down the side of the ridge to where they had parked in a clump of trees.

"That was about the hardest one to find that we've ever had." They congratulated each other.

"Yeah!" Said the other one. "Let's file this report and go have some lunch."

Sonny stayed still for what seemed a long time until he was sure they were gone. Perspiring heavily, he half hobbled, and tried to hurry up to the ridge. He knew when Lou came he would pick him up up there and he could tell him what happened. It was tough going. He stopped to catch his breath and looked up. The summit seemed miles away.

He ignored the stabbing pain across his chest but his legs felt as though he had a cement block tied around each one. The blood pounded in his head as he struggled on. He stopped to wipe the perspiration from his face, gave a deep gasp, clutched his chest, and died.

On his way back from Knoxville, Lou saw emergency vehicles, ambulances, the Sheriff's car and a few people milling around below at the water's edge as he drove over the river bridge. He wondered what had happened but he was in a rush to get up to the still with the corn and pick up Sonny.

Probably some kid playing in the river and got stuck, he thought. It's a bit chilly for swimming, though.

He drove on, his attention on the winding road again.

As he passed Bubba's store he could see that Charlie Keene was in there. He remembered being irritated when he discovered that Charlie had sold those two acres that adjoined Sonny's farm. There was no reasonable explanation as to why he didn't offer the land to Sonny before he sold it, other than, as Sonny always said, he didn't want to be next-door neighbors to the Cutter family. Odd, but that was over three years ago, just before Pa got hurt, he thought, and he had yet to meet the man from the north who bought it.

On up the road he went, casting side glances at Francie who was raking leaves in her front yard. He saw her look at him and he smiled and nodded as he passed, thinking he saw her wave to him.

"Was I dreaming?" he asked himself. "Did she wave, or even, smile? I would doubt it. She usually ignores me, just as she's done for years. I still want her, though. I guess I always will. Funny, I used to feel so sorry for her. Neither of her babies lived while Lottie and I had three healthy young 'uns. That must have been ol' Hodges' fault."

When he reached his driveway he swung the truck down the lane behind the barn and went up to the still the old way, coming out on the middle of the ridge, some distance down from the top.

Lou picked up the corn and headed right for the still. At first, he thought he would stop home and ask Leta to try to help Sonny a little more. On the way he changed his mind and decided to ask her that evening. For now, he wanted to get his pa home. He figured Sonny would be very tired by now. The bags of corn weighed one hundred pounds each so Lou went to the ridge a different way so he wouldn't have to carry them so far.

After he parked the pick-up in some trees he started down the hill, carrying a sack of corn. He hadn't gone far when he stumbled over Sonny's body. Horrified, he dropped the sack and knelt down over Sonny's lifeless form.

"Pa," he screamed. He rolled Sonny over but he knew right away there was no hope. He stood up, stunned, and almost ran down the ridge to the still. He saw that it had been completely destroyed. All except five jars full of liquid that the broken boiler's side hadn't shattered as it crashed to the ground.

Almost unconsciously, Lou picked up one of the jars nearest him and took a big swallow. He sat down on an overturned bucket.

"Pa," he said again. What he didn't realize was that he was drinking the initial distillate, full of methanol. It went right to his brain. He tried to think. He shook his head to try to get a clearer picture. They had all left him, his ma, Lottie, the boys,

Francie, but no matter how mean, cruel or ugly he could be, Sonny was always there. Lou stood up, shaky, now. He took another sip. He looked up at the mountaintop.

He shook his fist and cried, "You Mountains. You took everything from me and now, you took my Pa. You took what should have been mine, both the land and Francie, and gave it all to Hodges Clark." The brew influenced his reality. "Pa, I'll fix it for you. I'll get that Hodges Clark."

He kept a pistol and a rifle hidden in a tree trunk nearby. He staggered over, retrieved it and stumbled up the ridge. "I'll come back for you, Pa," he promised. "Hodges Clark," he called, "you're through taking what's mine. And if Francie doesn't come with me, I'll shoot her, too."

That struck him as funny and he laughed out loud as tears fell from his eyes.

"Francie," he cried, "You know it should have been me right from the start." His voice slurred.

He decided to climb to the top of his ridge, go down the other side to the Clark property and avenge his Pa although he would have to trudge through the deep fallen leaves and the underbrush. He staggered and tripped, fell and got up, only to fall again. Each time he fell, he blamed Hodges Clark for all of the problems in his life, totally unaware of how slurred his speech had become.

Blinded by his tears, almost insane from the methanol, he was near the summit when he stepped on a large branch. He gave it a hard kick to get it out of the way. Even in his stupor he realized it was a rattlesnake. He pulled the handgun out of his belt, forgot the safety catch was on and when it wouldn't fire he threw it at the snake. The snake coiled, jumped and bit him on the right leg just above his boot.

Lou saw it coming but he didn't feel the sting at first. He looked at the snake with amazement as it slithered away into the woods. He put the rifle down and, half sober now, limped over to a shagbark hickory, slid down the trunk and leaned against it as he sat on the cold, damp ground.

The pain gripped him. The motion helped circulate the venom through his body. Once it passed into his bloodstream it was even more devastating. The toxin caused swelling as the tissue died. Toxic waste from the dying cells caused bizarre side effects. There was a purple glow and a hiss. He passed out for about an hour, waking to an hallucination. He stared at his leg. It was three times its normal size and the swollen area was black. The pain was excruciating and getting stronger.

"If I sit here quietly it'll slow the venom down." It was his first rational thought in awhile. But it was too late. He knew no one would hear him if he yelled, so he just sat there. And died there. And Lou Cutter was no more.

A few days later, Rich Morris returned to the Cutter place. He knocked several times but no one answered the door. He went around to the barn and even to the 'bacca barn, but neither Lou nor Sonny were around, and he figured they may be up on the ridge, so he drove up the back way. He parked his truck in the usual place but didn't get out. There were rumors that the taxmen were in the area so he decided not to stay. He made a k-turn and left, stopping in at Bubba's on his way down the mountain.

"Hey, Rich, haven't seen you in awhile. Have a cup of coffee?" Bubba shook his hand.

Brinksy was playing cat and mouse. "Going up to Sonny's?"

"Thought I might. Just need a chaw of tobacco," He knew that they knew he was Sonny's partner. He also knew they could never prove anything.

"Nobody's to home." Brinksy was smiling. "Looks like the Cutter men have finally been caught."

"What do you mean?" Rich's eyes flashed, nervously.

"Postman says their mailbox is full. Guess they're in jail for running that still," Bubba supposed.

Rich played dumb. "What still?"

"Everybody on Stonesthrow knows they've been running a still all these years. If I were you I'd steer clear of them and their place for awhile." Brinksy just drank his coffee as he watched Rich's face. It reminded him of the look a deer had when it was caught in the headlights. He didn't say anything else.

"Well, I'll be," Rich tried to sound surprised, picked up his plug of tobacco, and nodded to the men as he left.

"Did you see his face?" Brinksy asked Bubba. "He won't be back for awhile."

"Yeah!" agreed Bubba, "if he does come back, he'll be caught next. I think he'll just go home to Hidden Hollow and we won't see him for a long time."

When the postman couldn't jam any more mail into the Cutter's rusty mailbox, he parked his truck at the entrance to the driveway and picked his way over the nails, random wood scraps and old bricks which lay in small piles here and there, and walked up to the house. Lou's truck was gone but there was an old Mustang parked alongside of the house. That was puzzling. The dogs were nowhere in sight, which made him very happy.

"Mr. Cutter. Sonny. Lou," he called

After three or four tries the front door finally opened and he was surprised to see young Billy Cutter standing there. Billy must have been sleeping. His shoulder-length hair was scraggly. He was barefoot wearing jeans and a tee shirt, and he resembled a young Sonny, right down to the surly, "Yeah?" that he spit out.

"Oh, it's you! When did you get out? I mean, when did you get home?" It was no secret that Billy had been in the Reformatory.

"I got in last night. What do you want?" He was abrupt, just like Sonny.

"Where's your Pa? The mailbox is overflowing"

"He ain't here. I ain't seen him since I got in. But then, he comes and goes." Billy was bored with the questions.

"Well, Leta usually gets the mail. Where is she?"

"Don't know that, either. Maybe they run off together." That struck Billy as preposterous and he gave a nasty chuckle, and then, laughed out loud.

The mailman wasn't amused. All of a sudden it made sense. The other day, he had read in the paper of an unnamed young woman who had thrown herself from the river bridge. He wanted to shake this selfish, arrogant kid. Before rage overtook him he turned and stumbled back through the debris, got into his truck and peeled down the winding road, leaving Billy standing on the porch.

The young man wondered why he left in such a storm. He shrugged his shoulders and went back into the house.

Deer season had started the day before he was freed and he planned to climb the ridge behind the house to scope out a good hiding place to get himself a buck. He hadn't meant to sleep so late but the bourbon he'd had the night before in Knoxville to celebrate his freedom had been pretty strong.

He laced up his boots, filled his canteen with water, and started up the ridge. It was steeper than he remembered it, and slow going through the leaves and underbrush. Near the top he almost tripped over something hard. When he leaned down to see what it was he recognized his Daddy's handgun. A few steps farther he came upon his daddy's rifle. Looking around, he finally saw his daddy's dead body, still slumped against the tree.

Billy stopped cold in his tracks for a moment, then turned and ran headlong down the ridge, avoiding the path to the still where his dead Grandpa's body lie, not stopping until he reached the house.

He emptied his Dad's sugar bowl of cash, ran outside, jumped in the Mustang a friend had lent him, spun wheels out of the driveway and headed towards Sevierville to get the

Sheriff. On the way, he thought better of it since he had just gotten out of jail, and made a sharp turn at the county highway, heading west. He never returned to Stonesthrow.

Bubba wrote to Junior with a sad heart, returning the money he had sent for him to put away for Leta, and also telling him that no one had seen his Pa or Grandpa in a while and that they could only conclude that the still had been raided and they were in jail. Bubba said he'd try to find out where they were and let him know. He never did.

Junior stayed in the Army for twenty years. Stationed in Germany most of that time, he married a German girl and they had one son. When he retired from the Army they moved to Florida where he opened a Laundromat business, eventually owning five stores.

When Jack grew up he became an over-the-road truck driver. He was delivering a load of furniture down Mt. Harrison when the load shifted, forcing the truck over the edge. He spent the rest of his life in a nursing home.

Since no one claimed their land it was redeemed by the county for back taxes. The county gave it to the state who offered it to the National Park. The buildings were removed and the expanse was added to the boundary of the scenic Foothills Parkway.

In nineteen seventy, just after the Christmas holiday season, Francie, Marybelle and Evelyn began planning for the next annual neighborhood picnic. They met at Francie's and agreed they wanted it to be like it was in the old days. They made arrangements to have it at the church grounds and sent the invitations out early so everyone would have time to adjust his or her schedule.

In late June, Stonesthrow resounded with the lively music of Billy Mann and his Stony Mountain Boys, a group beginning to have national prominence. They all came. Lem

Clark, who turned sixty-five that year, flew in from California with Mrs. Clark and their daughter, Kaye. Annie, their rodeo rider, came with her husband, Ray, all the way from Calgary, Canada. Hodges' twin sisters, Alice and Loretta, their husbands and all of their children, as well as Carol Crewe Budzinski, her husband, Jim, and their two boys came up from the valley.

Ada, Duncan and Mrs. Crewe came with Ada's three children. Marybelle and Charlie's widowed son, Eddie, with his two boys, drove over from Nashville, and Evelyn and Tom Brinks's brood came from Knoxville.

Mr. and Mrs. Mann were in Italy for a week after visiting their son, Ralph, who was stationed in the Mediterranean with the Navy. They promised to stop on their way back to Oklahoma.

"Now, this is more like it, "Evelyn smiled at Marybelle as they watched the youngsters run and play while the older folks danced.

"Just like it used to be." Marybelle said. "It seems like we're still one big happy family."

Francie and Hodges stood, arm in arm, watching the group from the sidelines. "This is what Stonesthrow is all about," Francie said, hugging Hodges.

"I want to make a toast," Hodges said. He tapped on his iced tea glass until he had everyone's attention. He looked up at the Great Smoky Mountains all around them. These mountains had brought life in all of its facets and there was still a lot of living to do. He raised his glass.

"To Stonesthrow."

THE END

Printed in the United States
90749LV00003B/133-141/A